JACK ALWAYS SEEKS HIS FORTUNE

JACK ALWAYS SEEKS HIS FORTUNE

Authentic Appalachian Jack Tales

DONALD DAVIS

August House Publishers, Inc.
LITTLE ROCK

Published by August House, Inc.,
P.O. Box 3223, Little Rock, Arkansas, 72203,
501-372-5450.

Printed in the United States of America

10 9 8 7 6 5 4 3 2 1

LIBRARY OF CONGRESS CATALOGING-IN-PUBLICATION DATA

Davis, Donald D., 1944–
Jack always seeks his fortune: authentic Appalachian Jack tales / Donald Davis. —
1st ed.
p.   cm.
Summary: A collection of thirteen Jack tales from the southern Appalachian Mountains,
including "The Time Jack Told a Big Tale," "The Time Jack Cured the Doctor," and
"The Time Jack Stole the Cows."
ISBN 0-87483-281-0 (alk. paper) : $19.95
ISBN 0-87483-280-2 (pbk.: alk. paper) : $9.95
1. Tales—Appalachian Region.
[1. Folklore—Appalachian Region.] I. Title.
PZ8.1.D289Jac   1992
398.21'097568—dc20   92-25026

First Edition, 1992

Executive editor: Liz Parkhurst
Project editor: Tom Baskett, Jr.
Design director: Ted Parkhurst
Cover illustration and design: Harvill-Ross Studios, Ltd.
Typography: Lettergraphics / Little Rock

This book is printed on archival-quality paper which meets the
guidelines for performance and durability of the Committee on
Production Guidelines for Book Longevity of the
Council on Library Resources.

AUGUST HOUSE, INC.   PUBLISHERS   LITTLE ROCK

For my mother,
Lucille Walker Davis

Acknowledgments

THE SOURCES OF THESE STORIES in my own memory go so far back as to be indistinguishable from the very Appalachian context of my early life. A strong part of that context was the presence of my maternal grandparents, Grady and Zephie Walker, especially my grandmother. In thankfulness I remember them.

My appreciation, however, goes back much farther than that. To the generations of storytellers who talked old Jack down through the years and across the miles and the waters from the British highlands to those of North Carolina, I am forever grateful.

In a different direction, I am thankful to those who want to hear and read about Jack in the present day. The encouragement of people who are excited and strengthened in their own life journeys when they meet Jack as a new friend has inspired me to work at sharing my knowledge of him instead of merely keeping it in my own mind. Without all these persons, the stories would likely have lived and died in my own memory.

I wish to thank especially and personally my mother, who helped to raise Jack in my own mind; my wife, Merle Smith Davis, who helps me keep him alive and healthy now; Ted and Liz Parkhurst, and Kathleen Harper of August House, who are giving him a new life through the publication of this collection; and, lastly, thanks to Joseph Sobol, who explains Jack to those who didn't get to grow up with him.

A special word of appreciation goes to my friends Ray and Rosa Hicks. My Jack lives in my memory, but, if I want to go see how Jack is doing today, I will find him well cared for and living at Ray and Rosa's house.

Contents

The Jack Tales: Coming From Afar

*A*t some point in their reading, most educated folks will run
across the name of Jack, and of "the Jack tales"—an intrigu-
ingly complex phrase, evoking in one breath the humility of the
commonplace and the grandeur of art. If they are much luckier,
they may even meet up with someone who is able to *tell* these
stories, with all the rich, personal nuance that flows from immer-
sion in a particular local tradition.

It is something like stumbling upon a mountain stream.
You can lose yourself in the play of light and shade along the
surface. You can taste the clear, cold water. Eventually you can
follow the stream to where it joins up with many others, a living,
flowing system that we call the oral tradition; and finally you
can watch it return to the sea, that source and destination which
the ancient writers called "The Ocean of Story."

For Richard Chase, the discovery occurred one day in the
spring of 1935. Here's how he described it to an interviewer,
forty years later:

> During the Depression, there was a great meeting in
> Raleigh: Emergency Relief in Education. There were about
> seven hundred teachers there. I was to lead singing.
> And there was an old lady, near there, that I had visited.
> She knew ballads and so forth. And I went and got her. And

we brought her to this big meeting in Raleigh. And she sang, and sang, and sang.

And afterwards, Marshall P. Ward...came up to me and said that *his* people knew old tales, "handed down from generation to generation like you said about the songs that woman was a-singing'."

"Old tales?"

"Yeah."

"What're they about?"

"Eh, they're mostly about a boy named Jack."

Immediately, you'd think, "Jack and the Beanstalk?"

And Marshall Ward said, "No. That's the way it's in them library books. We don't tell 'em thataway." And somehow I knew *at once,* I'd hit on a *live* oral tradition of tales, the same as Mr. Sharp got for his big thick volume, *English Folksongs from the Southern Appalachians;* some songs he found over here that'd been forgotten in England, you see.

So, I finally visited Marshall Ward's father and uncle, with a big yellow tablet; no tape recorders or nothin'. And took about seven years going in and out of Beech Mountain, a-scratchin' 'em down.[1]

Marshall Ward introduced Chase and—through Chase's books—the world to the flourishing tale-telling traditions of the North Carolina mountains. These wonder tales, or Maerchen as they were called by the Brothers Grimm (the broad German term is still used by international scholars), had been brought to the Southern Appalachians by the first European settlers at the end of the eighteenth century. At that time, the stories would have been common property among folk of English, Scottish, Irish, German, or French ancestry all over the new nation. They were a natural form of recreation and entertainment among people whose contact with the printed word was limited, whose days were hard and filled with toil, and whose nights were long and dark. The need to light up those long nights with astonishing scenes and daredevil journeys, made safe and familiar by the soft wind of the storyteller's breath, kept the tales vividly alive.

It cannot be over-emphasized that these are *oral* tales, designed to be told and retold aloud. They have simple, repetitive structures, and feature striking visual images which imprint themselves easily on the listening mind. The plots and incidents of the stories are immemorially ancient, some going back many thousands of years. They have changed their outer garments over the centuries as they pass back and forth across cultural and geographical boundaries, yet the story essences remain as recognizable and eternally renewing as the face of the moon.

During the nineteenth century these long oral tales began to die out in the towns and lowland settlements where access to the world was greater and the daily requirement of distraction easier to fill. Yet in parts of the Southern mountains, where isolation and intensive family ties provided occasions for the stories to be passed along, they endured undisturbed.

The spread of television in the fifties and sixties was the most serious threat yet to the tradition even in the mountain strongholds. But at the same time as the structure of the rural community and even the rural night-time was being assaulted by the electronic "Global Village," popular revivals of interest in traditional arts—first, in the sixties, in folk music, and then, in the seventies and eighties, in storytelling—have brought new generations of tellers and listeners to Old Jack, his brothers Will and Tom, and to their cousins in related storytelling traditions from around the world.

Let's look more closely here at Jack, the character, and the cycle of stories that bears his name.

In the storytelling traditions of many peoples there are key figures acting as story-magnets. These figures draw to themselves great portions of floating folklore material. Often these story-magnets are trickster figures, like the native American Coyote or the Afro-American Brer Rabbit. Or they can be the trickster's foil, the numbskull, as in the German-American Eulenspijjel or the Foolish Irishman cycles. In other cases they fill heroic roles, like the Irish Finn MacCool or Kullervo of the

Finnish Kalevala. In America these figures were particularly likely to be fit into cycles of tall tales, like those featuring the braggart-heroes Davy Crockett, Mike Fink, or Gib Morgan. There are trickster figures on the more "adult" levels of culture who also become centers of folktale cycles: Ireland's Daniel O'Connell is one; so is the slave John in the Afro-American John and Old Master cycle; and so in his way is the travelling salesman of party-joke fame.

The Appalachian Jack tale cycle has something in common with all these types. In some tales, Jack is a fool and a laughingstock ("The Time Jack Went to Seek His Fortune," "The Time Jack Got His First Job"); in others, he succeeds by cleverness where the strong fail ("The Time Jack Stole the Cows"); in still others, he wins by perseverance, humility, and magical assistance ("The Time Jack Learned About Old and New," "The Time Jack Got the Wishing Ring"); and he even figures in tall tales ("The Time Jack Told a Big Tale" or "Jack's Hunting Trip" from Chase's collection[2]). Several of the Jack tales that Donald Davis heard from his uncle Frank Davis fall into the adult trickster mode, the genre known to folklorists as the fabliau ("The Time Jack Fooled the Miller," "The Time Jack Cured the Doctor"). "The Time Jack Solved the Hardest Riddle" is an Appalachian version of a medieval romance, known in Chaucer's version as "The Wife of Bath's Tale," or the fifteenth-century *The Weddynge of Sir Gawen and Dame Ragnell*.[3] And the popularity of Jack as a figure in English nursery rhymes shows yet another facet of his folkloric significance.

There are Jack tales, too, in which Jack takes on the mythic attributes of a shaman, or culture hero, by moving freely between natural and spiritual worlds, subduing evil, restoring harmony, and bringing back blessings to the community. "The Time Jack Got the Wishing Ring" ("Old Fire Dragoman" in Chase) has been associated with Beowulf, the hero of the transitional epic of early Christian England.[4] The Beech Mountain tale "Hardy Hardhead"[5] was once woven around the Irish hero Finn Mac-

Cool; and "Cat and Mouse"[6] parallels the Biblical story of Joseph. Even "Jack and the Beanstalk" contains the basic pattern of the shamanic journey. Donald Davis's "The Time Jack Went Up in the Big Tree" develops that same pattern in much deeper, darker detail, into one of the longest, rarest, and most mysterious of American wonder tales.[7] And "The First Time Jack Came to America," which concludes this volume, precisely parallels the Welsh legend of Taliesin (from the *Mabinogion).* Taliesin came to be known as the founder of Welsh bardic poetry, only after being swallowed by, and reborn to, the hag Ceridwen. Jack, in Donald's version, is similarly twice-born, then borne on the ocean, the womb of all life, and reborn naked on the New World shore, with all of the wisdom of the Old World intact inside him: a startling image of the luminous, immigrant American potential.[8]

Most languages and cultures, particularly those in the Indo-European community, have their own stories and characters related to the Jack tales and Jack. Always the stories and the character take on protective coloration from the surrounding culture. This is at the heart of the cycle's enduring power. Jack is a universal type; yet because of his broadness of definition he lends himself to localization, so that people in widely divergent settings could feel, as Donald Davis did as a child, that "Jack was a boy, just like we were.... I had the feeling that Jack could just walk right in."[9]

Jack, as a matter of fact, is less of an individualized character than an emblem of human potential in many of its representative stages. This open, indeterminate nature helped to make Jack an ideal vessel in which to blend the wandering narrative traditions of Appalachia. It also makes it possible for Jack to be conceived of in entirely different cultural contexts: for example, by African-American storytellers, as in the Jack tales collected by Zora Neale Hurston in Florida,[10] by Guy Carawan in the Carolina Sea Islands,[11] and in Jackie Torrence's spirited performances; or in the context of small-town America after the

Second World War, as in filmmaker Tom Davenport's recent adaptation of Chase's "Soldier Jack."[12] In my own storytelling I have occasionally cast Jack as a boy from suburbia, or as a Vietnam veteran, while retaining the motifs and structures of the traditional tales. The stories change, as we change; yet their essence, like our human essence, endures.

Our familiar Appalachian Jack, we can safely say, has his roots in Germany and the British Isles. His name is a diminutive form of John, as the German equivalent, Hans, is a diminutive form of Johannes. The name itself can yield interesting insights into the character and its lasting fascination.

John is descended from a Hebrew name, Johannon, which the *Oxford English Dictionary* interprets as "Jah (God) is gracious." The name John spread throughout Europe with the coming of Christianity. It was a common name in England a century after the Norman Conquest. The nickname Jack was first recorded there in the thirteenth century, and grew so popular that it shortly came to connote the very essence of commonness itself ("every man-jack of them"). In this way, the name has gone on to be applied in a host of related senses—its entries run for four packed pages in the *Oxford English Dictionary*.

The general theme of all of them is *personification*. Jack has served to personify almost any salient trait, be it maleness (jack-deer, man-jack), usefulness (windowjack, tire-jack), coldness (Jack Frost), smallness (Jack Sprat). Any average group of children could add to the list. Jack has come to personify Hallowe'en, and by extension the dead (Jack-o'-Lantern), the Navy (Jack Tar), various species of mammal (jackrabbit, jackass), bird (jackdaw), and plant (jack-in-the-pulpit). It also, significantly, in view of the tales that bear the name, has been used to personify the trickster ("jack-knave"), both in slang usage ("He played the jack with me" or "Don't jack me around") and in the common deck of playing cards, where it also represents the son.

Generally speaking, then, Jack has become a sign in English for Everyman, and beyond that, for the male principle in any of its lowly or earthy expressions. Borne as a talisman, the name carries the savor of divine abundance and grace ("God is gracious"), and a natural affinity for all creation. Perhaps this is part of the unformed truth behind the statement of old Sam Harmon, a cousin of Marshall Ward, Ray Hicks, and the other Beech Mountain tellers, who told folklorist Herbert Halpert, "If I were to name my boys over, I'd name all of them Jack. I never knowed a Jack but what was lucky."[13]

I first had the good luck to hear Donald Davis tell a Jack tale in the early 1980s, on the Swapping Ground of the National Storytelling Festival in Jonesborough, Tennessee. I was a graduate student in folklore at the University of North Carolina at the time, and Donald was just emerging as a leader in the nationwide storytelling revival. The story he was telling (here titled "The Time Jack Told a Big Tale") had never been collected as a Jack tale in the United States, although I had come across parallel versions from the British Isles.[14] When, in talking with Donald afterwards, I found out that he had learned this and many other equally rare stories from his family's oral traditions, I felt my fledgling folklorist's nape-hair stand straight up.

It was this same kind of excitement that Chase must have felt at that meeting in 1935. Donald's storytelling greatly extended the repertoire and filled in our (outsiders') understanding of this cycle of tales and its hero. His family, of Scottish and Welsh descent, had settled in the mountains in the eighteenth century, eighty miles down the Blue Ridge from the Beech Mountain families of tellers, and the tales that Donald inherited had a sweep and a Celtic wildness all their own. Also his reflective involvement in the *process* of story performance, memory, and creativity could bring forth essential insights into his tale-telling tradition.

Yet there were important differences, too, in the context of our meeting. The world has changed greatly since 1935, and the discipline of folklore has had to come along. I was being given an opportunity to study the Jack tale tradition in transition—and also to negotiate a new kind of relationship between folklorist and "folk" artist.

It was common practice among folklore collectors of Richard Chase's day to appropriate the tales, songs, and dances they published under their own names, sealing them with the cultural authority of print. "Informants," in this ethos, were treated as necessary tools for the construction of the ethnographic writer's own authority. In part, at least, this was a function of that "big yellow tablet," which neither inspired, required, nor even allowed a traditional performer's own creativity or expressive style to be precisely recorded. In the case of fluid folklore forms like the folktale, this led either to bare summaries of plot lines, as in the earliest Jack tales collected in North Carolina in the twenties by Isabel Gordon Carter,[15] or to freely edited retellings in a ventriloquist-author's voice, as in *The Jack Tales* and *Grandfather Tales*.

With the continual advance of audio, then video technology, the ethos of the folklore field advanced as well. The ideal of a folklore text expanded to encompass a more and more minute representation of the storyteller's style. This, we now know, goes well beyond exact wording to explore questions of rhythm, timing, gesture, and relationship to audience and surroundings, even to the inner environment of the performer's relationship with tradition and with self.

All these questions have increasingly thrust the individual traditional artist and his or her social milieu into the foreground of folklore studies. They have recast the folklorist in the role of recording technician, transcriber, and, at best, creative partner in a cross-cultural dialogue on the workings of oral tradition. The academic folklorist's chief source of power has lain in the production of books and recordings, through controlling the technological and analytical frames within which the performer is to be perceived. Another, more esoteric function for the folklorist in the "public sector" has become the manipulation of state and federal funding agencies, in order to bring these technologies within folk artists' ken.

But Donald Davis has little need of any such academic or public intervention. He has long produced recordings in astonishing abundance and with apparent effortlessness, as if to make an outstanding commercial storytelling tape were as easy for him as standing still and talking. Now he is applying that same naturalness and ease to the making of books.

Over a period of several years, through several interviews and innumerable performance occasions, I had the opportunity to follow Donald about, observing him at work and prying into his repertoire and his creative process. What I received was an education, and, it also happened, the material for a master's thesis. What Donald received was mainly the opportunity to exercise patience.

Donald is at home in the contemporary world of the storytelling revival, yet his memory is steeped in an ancient world of tales. That no other folklorist had yet studied his storytelling seemed incredible to me at the time. As I wrote then, it was like a purloined letter, sitting open under the eyes of researchers who yet kept blindly combing dark hollers and the endless shade of library stacks. Yet now I can appreciate, too, the simple effectiveness of his disguise.

Donald Davis's art is based almost entirely on traditional themes, forms and techniques; yet his approach to it is highly personal, reflective, and creative, and he has adapted it to contexts which carry few of the outward signs of tradition. The stories and their backgrounds are his own, yet he is involved in a lifelong work of restoring and reshaping them in order to make them, and the values he derives from them, available to a wider community. He has moved beyond the boundaries of his local tradition, much as musicians like Jean Ritchie or Hedy West have brought their family traditions to urban listeners, borne on a swell of transcultural hunger.

Despite the stigma it has received from academic purists, cultural revivalism needs to be recognized as a natural psychic behavior in the face of rapid social change. Recent works like Hobsbawm and Ranger's *The Invention of Tradition* and Henry Glassie's *All Silver and No Brass* have explored some of the myriad ways that folk traditions have been restored to meet the needs of a changing community.[16] We might even see that the development of the Jack tale tradition in Appalachia was a result of an analogous process, albeit working in reverse: storytellers from several different ethnic and traditional stocks settled together in isolated areas, and rewove their various tale traditions around the unifying figure of Jack.

As he carries Jack out of a vanishing rural South and into the schools and auditoriums of scattered, pre-millennial American communities, Donald Davis's role in the present storytelling revival is a pivotal one. Throughout his repertoire, and in his workshops and his writings, he remains a key example and spokesman for the oral-traditional approach to the art. Whether his stories have actually been passed down intact in his traditional community, or have been reconstructed after a lapse of decades, or have been woven himself from memory and imagination, they are all developed, stored, and re-created through what Donald calls a "picture-centered approach"— which he opposes to the "word-centered approach" of oral-interpretive performers.

Donald holds that stories are preserved in his memory, not in words and sentences, but in images and sequences of images. As Joseph Campbell wrote, "The folk tale is the primer of the picture-language of the Soul."[17] The key for Donald, just as for Jack and the old king in "The Time Jack Told a Big Tale," is to "see it in his mind":

> What is the biggest difference between the way I learned stories and learning from a book? Well, the biggest difference is that I never learned a story, I just soaked it up. What that means is that by hearing the same story told over and over in

slightly different ways, what you finally absorb is not one particular version of a story, but instead the underlying picture. Telling a story like that is telling about a part of yourself as familiar as the warts on your body.... Remembering the words is irrelevant, because, once you have the picture in your mind, you can describe it many different ways until you see that the people who are listening see it too.[18]

So, if the text is *not* the actual story, what *are* these texts, enclosed within these covers? They are just that: texts—graceful, idiomatically-rendered texts, each of which amounts to one particular performance of a given story, keyed for the infinitely repeatable context of an absent performer and an active reader.

Donald had begun to try and set these stories down on paper long before I met him. But the act of freezing the stories in written forms often had chilling effects on his own fluid inner process of maintaining the stories orally. At the very least, he found he could not go back and read what he had written, for fear of inhibiting his spontaneous oral creativity.

We had talked for several years about collaborating on a book of transcriptions of oral performances of these stories. These would have been faithful documentations of the live performance context; but, ironically, they would have been less faithful to the actual, intended context of the tales—the leisurely converse of reader and book.

In the course of preparing his first two volumes of original and traditional stories for August House, Donald Davis has developed an increasing ease of technique in crafting literary performances to mirror the warmth, wisdom, and directness of his spoken ones. In his mastery of these often divided media, Donald has seized back the technological reins from even the best-intentioned ethnographer.

For students interested in comparing the texts of oral and written versions, he has graciously agreed to let a performance of "The Time Jack Told a Big Tale" be transcribed for a forthcoming scholarly anthology of Jack tales. For the rest, I am purely delighted to know that one of the most accomplished and versatile tellers of traditional stories in America today is bringing another facet of his dazzling repertoire to the printed page, like his hero, on his own.

—Joseph Daniel Sobol

Notes

1. Interview recorded 10 April 1975 at Berea College, Kentucky.

2. Richard Chase, *The Jack Tales* (Boston: Houghton Mifflin, 1943), 151–60, 198–99n.

3. Joseph Campbell, *Hero With A Thousand Faces* (Princeton: Bollingen Foundation, 1949), 118n.

4. Chase, 106ff., 194.

5. Ibid., 96ff., 194.

6. Ibid., 127ff., 197–98.

7. Linda Degh, "The Tree that Reached Up to the Sky (type 468)," in *Studies in East European Folk Narrative,* ed. Linda Degh (Bloomington: American Folklore Society and Indiana University Folklore Series, 1978), 263–316; also see Sandor Erdesz, "The World-View of Lajos Ami," in *Sacred Narrative: Readings in the Theory of Myth,* ed. Alan Dundes (Berkeley and Los Angeles: Univ. of California, 1984), 315–35.

8. Lady Charlotte Guest, trans., *The Mabinogion, from the Welsh of the Llyfr Coch o Hergest (The Red Book of Hergest)* (London, 1877); also see Campbell, 239–43.

9. Donald Davis, personal interview, High Point, NC, 30 January 1985.

10. Zora Neale Hurston, *Mules and Men* (Bloomington: Indiana Univ. Press), 51–58.

11. Guy and Candie Carawan, eds., *Been in the Storm So Long.* L.P., Folkways FS3842.

12. Tom Davenport, *Soldier Jack.* (Delaplane, VA: Davenport Films, 1988). Film.

13. Chase, 187.

14. Katherine Briggs, *A Dictionary of British Folktales in the English Language; Part A: Folk Narratives* (London: Routledge and Kegan Paul, 1970), 2: 424.

15. Isabel Gordon Carter, "Mountain White Folklore: Tales from the Southern Blue Ridge." *Journal of American Folklore* 38 (1925): 341–68.

16. Eric Hobsbawm and Terence Ranger, *The Invention of Tradition* (Cambridge, Eng.: Cambridge Univ. Press, 1983); Henry Glassie, *All Silver and No Brass* (Bloomington: Indiana Univ. Press, 1975).

17. Joseph Campbell, "Folkloristic Commentary," in *The Complete Grimm's Fairy Tales* (New York: Pantheon, 1944), 864.

18. Donald D. Davis and Kay Stone, "'To Ease the Heart': Traditional Storytelling." *Storytelling Journal* 1, no. 1 (1984): 3–6.

NOTE: *Parts of this introduction have appeared in different forms in the following works: Everyman and Jack: The Storytelling of Donald Davis, master's thesis, University of North Carolina, 1987; "Jack of a Thousand Faces," in From the Brothers Grimm (2, no. 1 [1988]), reprinted in Storytelling (1, no. 1 [1989]); and "Between Worlds: Donald Davis's 'Jack's Biggest Tale,'" from Jack in Two Worlds: Jack Tales in Performance (forthcoming, Publications of the American Folklore Society).*

I Grew Up Close to Jack

When I was growing up in the Haywood County mountains of western North Carolina, I was totally unaware that I was hearing a large number of traditional stories not generally known by other American children. In fact, I was not even aware that what would later be called "storytelling" was taking place all around me daily.

The word "storytelling" was neither used nor avoided. It simply was not a part of the vocabulary in that part of the world. What I was hearing was just "talking." The closest I heard people come to putting a label on this particular kind of talking came when someone should say, "Tell about that time when ..." "Telling a story" was more like a polite way of referring to prevarication than a label for some established, identifiable oral ritual.

But the stories were there. The talking was full of them. I remember having great pleasure in just hanging around my grandparents' front porch so that I could listen to the old people "just talk."

I do recall one occasion as an elementary school student when we had a school-wide assembly program in which a man played a little wooden pipe and entertained us with songs and stories. My parents later asked me what the man talked about. My answer was that he talked about Jack but didn't tell about anything that we didn't know. And—I reported—he didn't get some of it right.

The man's name, I also remembered, was Richard Chase, later known to me as the collector and editor of the Beech Mountain Jack tales.

Many years later, as a college English student, I began to make a series of interesting discoveries. When we read Chaucer, I already knew many of the stories. "The Miller's Tale," "The Reeve's Tale," "The Wife of Bath's Tale" I already knew in substance. When we read Shakespeare, I had already heard the story around which "King Lear" centered. The characters and the settings were different, but the story lines were the same. I had heard them, mostly as stories about Jack, when I was growing up.

With a revived national interest in storytelling building throughout the 1970s, I began to re-examine my memory and family associations, actively searching for those previously unnoticed stories of childhood. I discovered that I could put back together nearly forty traditional tales, most of them about Jack. Before I ever began to tell original stories, I worked to remember the setting and content of Jack and his adventures.

The storytelling I grew up with was part of the fabric of daily living. Most of it went on while the adults around me did their chores and led their children into doing the same. Storytelling was the oral accompaniment to cooking, housekeeping, gardening, feeding, milking—all these jobs and others performed not to the accompaniment of a radio, but, rather, to the sounds of talking. Grandmother could tell about Jack no matter what she was doing.

I do not remember stories being labeled for entertainment, nor do I recall setting times aside for storytelling. Such talk just naturally occurred after dinner or perhaps on a picnic or other outing. Storytelling was more likely the accompaniment for stringing beans when there was no television or radio.

Jack became a very real person to me as I heard of his fortune-seeking over and over again. There was a time when I was convinced that he was a boy who surely lived just around the mountain from my grandmother's house. I imagined asking Grandmother to take me to meet Jack, but some unknown knowledge that his reality surpassed singular embodiment kept me from asking the question to spare myself the disappointment. My request was simply that Grandmother tell me about what Jack had been doing lately.

While my Grandmother Walker was the person who told most of the stories I remember, there were other stories which, like jokes, seemed to belong to the whole community and were told by whoever thought of them at the time. Most of these stories I heard again and again so that my memory is now of the story more strongly than of the telling.

In the early days of my own storytelling career, I did not make much use of this knowledge of Jack tales. I still had the feeling that everyone knew these stories and that adults especially would not sit still for them. I have begun to discover, however, that most children do not know Jack very well, and I find myself telling about him more and more.

Out of nearly three dozen Jack tales which I can recall, most presented in this collection have, I believe, either not been published in their Appalachian manifestations or are so different from any extant version as to make comparison interesting rather than repetitious. The deliberate exception to this principle is "The Time Jack Got His First Job," a common tale included so that those acquainted with the genre may compare it and the "Lazy Jack" versions they know.

My final wish behind this collection is to present a collection of stories about Jack put together, perhaps for the first time, by someone who grew up with Jack inside that oral tradition.

My impression of the prior collections made by folklorists and outside collectors is that the imposition of time restraints (often an element in collecting) has greatly altered the stories themselves. This trying to find as many stories as possible in the shortest time has resulted in tellers, who perceived that hurry, telling *about* the stories rather than telling the stories as people who lived with Jack daily would do, soaking slowly in his tales without any concern about how long they lasted or whether they would even be finished on a particular occasion. I see those early story summaries as being characteristic of cases in which tellers were, for the first time, being asked to tell strangers about Jack.

My desire is to tell about Jack as I remember living with his stories, without hurry, without concern for shaping tales for the outside listener.

Upon reflection, I am aware that the stories about Jack which I heard came at a time when the first members of my ancestral families were beginning, through reading and education, to have contact with a world beyond their own. I am convinced that Jack was so important to them as the center of all story that *every* tale they told was about Jack, regardless of where it had come from. I can easily hear storytellers of my childhood tell the story of the Good Samaritan about Tom and Will and Jack rather than about the priest, the Levite, and the Samaritan. I can also hear the Prodigal Son told about Jack leaving home while the older brothers stay home.

It is therefore probable that during this very period of first exposure to the world as a whole, these old stories picked up elements from sources far beyond the Appalachian roots which were much purer a generation earlier. This slice of time in the Jack tradition may in itself be interesting, for it is a period when the form of the story often seemed more important than its specific content.

In part, this means that Jack is not always politically correct in terms of today's world. My difficult choice has been to leave

Jack as he was rather than trying to make him into someone we might think he should have been.

After all, recording any storytelling tradition is a sacred act of describing a living past, not an attempt at prescribing the future.

—*Donald Davis*

The Time Jack Went to Seek His Fortune

*Almost every story that I ever heard about Jack is a story in which he is seeking his fortune in one way or another. The natural beginning place for this collection, then, is with a story in which the word **fortune** plays the major part. This is a story which, in these days of the 1990s, might be called a "Zen Jack tale."*

One time Jack was living alone with his mother. They were living in a poor little log house way up in the mountains and having a hard time just keeping warm and not starving to death. Jack's daddy wasn't there, and Jack's big brothers Tom and Will had already gone off from home to look for their fortunes. Jack wasn't much help at home, and so he and his mother really were getting along quite poorly.

One day Jack came to his mother and told her his plan. "Mama," he said, "we're having such a hard time that I think it's about time for me to get on out of here and seek my fortune. Tom and Will must have found their fortunes because they never have come back home, and I think that it is just time for me to look for mine."

"That's a pretty good idea, Jack," his mother said. "You have to do it sometime, and it might as well be now."

So Jack's mother packed up a clean shirt and a little sack of food to start him on the way to seek his fortune. After breakfast the next day, Jack started out walking down the road.

There was just one problem. All of a sudden Jack realized that he didn't know what a fortune was. All he knew was that his big brothers had left home to seek theirs, and if they had done it, he could do it, too. So he was looking, but he didn't know what he was looking for.

Jack thought, "Well, I don't know what my fortune is, but I guess I'll recognize it when I see it." He went walking on along, farther and farther from home, looking under every bush and behind every house and barn. He looked through the countryside and then all through town, and he never did see anything that he thought looked like his fortune.

By the time two days of this wandering had passed, Jack had dirtied both of his traveling shirts and had eaten up all of the food that his mother had sent with him. He thought, "I'm going to starve to death before I ever find my fortune. I guess I'll have to stop looking for a while and get a job so I can eat."

Jack began looking for work from house to house, and before long he found a farmer who was in need of a helper.

"You're in luck, Jack!" the farmer said. "You can work for me, and besides that you can sleep right here in our house and even eat right here at the table with us. Why, my wife will even wash your shirts for you right along when we wash ours."

Jack surely was pleased by this. At least now he wouldn't starve to death.

The farmer went on talking. "Since you're going to eat and sleep right here, you won't need any money, Jack. So I'll just save up what I ought to pay you, and then when you're ready to go on your own way, I'll pay you for the time you've worked here all at once. That ought to help you out."

Jack didn't care one way or the other about this part. He had left home to start with because he was starving to death. If he was going to have food and a sleeping place, well, he just wouldn't need any money.

Jack got along very well at the farmer's house. The farmer's wife treated him just like he was one of hers. He worked there for a week, and then for a month, and then stayed right on through the winter and even fattened up a little bit.

Before Jack knew it, he had worked and eaten and slept at the farmer's house for a full year and was not even interested in leaving. In all this time, Jack had not seen one cent of real money for his pay.

Well, the time just went on and on like that until one day Jack woke up and realized that he had been working for the farmer for *seven years*.

He sat up in bed and said right out loud to himself, "I've got to get out of here! I left home to seek my fortune, and this *job* is purely holding me up. Why, I'll never find my fortune if I have to keep working! I've gotten seven years behind already. I better get on out of here."

So Jack told the farmer and his wife that he would be leaving the next day so he could get on his way looking for his fortune.

They were sad to see him go. After all, he had pretty well grown up right in their house. But the farmer told him if he was determined to quit work to seek his fortune he would have all of his pay for the seven years of work ready for him at breakfast the next morning.

That night Jack packed up a few clothes and things he had accumulated during his time at the farmer's house. He realized that he still didn't know what a fortune was, but once he got rid of this job that was holding him up, at least he would be better dressed to look for it.

Jack went down to breakfast the next morning, and right there in the middle of the kitchen floor he saw a two-bushel basket just filled to the brim with money. There were some dollar bills, but it was mostly quarters and dimes and nickels. Why, Jack figured that basket of money had to weigh over five hundred pounds just to begin with. He had never seen so much money in his life. At least he wouldn't starve to death while he was looking for his fortune.

After breakfast Jack started trying to move that basket of money out to the road so he could get on his way.

It took all day. He pulled and pushed and shoved and strained until by lunch time he had it out the door and down the steps into the yard. After a little rest, it took Jack the entire afternoon to get the basket of money on out to the side of the road.

Just about dark Jack went back up to the farmer's house. "I'm not making much progress," he told the farmer. "All that money you gave me is holding me up. Unless I can find some way to get rid of it, why, I will never be able to get on with looking for my fortune!"

Jack spent one last night at the farmer's house. He didn't sleep much, though. He was up most of the night trying to figure out how to get rid of the money.

Next morning he said goodbye for the second time, went out to the side of the road, and sat down beside the money to think for a while.

In about an hour he heard someone coming down the road and looked up to see a man approaching in a two-wheeled buggy pulled by a pretty fine-looking horse. Jack had an idea. "If I had a horse and buggy like that, I really would be able to get on to seeking my fortune."

So Jack waved to the man in the buggy and got him to stop. "Hello!" he said. "Would you be willing to swap that horse and buggy for this basket of money I've got here? Took me seven years to earn it, but it's keeping me from seeking my fortune. What I really need is that horse and buggy."

The traveler looked at the basket of money and realized that there was enough there to buy a good team of horses and a brand-new four-wheeled buggy. He looked at Jack and said, "Well, I guess I'd be willing to trade with you. Would it be an even swap?"

"Only if you take every last cent of this money, "Jack said. "I've just got to get rid of it!"

And so Jack took off down the road in his horse and buggy while the traveler sat down beside the road and happily started counting his new money.

After a few days Jack realized that he had made a mistake. Not only was he making no progress at all in figuring out what his fortune might look like, but he was having to find food for his new horse as well as for himself. It was a terrible amount of trouble.

"I've got to get rid of this horse and buggy," he thought out loud. "They are no help at all and are really holding me up from looking for my fortune."

The next day he was going down the road when he met a woman who was leading a cow to town to sell it.

"Now, *that* is what I need," Jack thought. "If I had that cow, I would have plenty of milk to drink, and the cow would just eat grass along the side of the road and feed herself. Besides that, I'll bet I could ride her once in a while if I get tired."

Jack stopped when he got to the woman with the cow. "Hello," he said. "Where are you going with that cow?"

"Why, I'm taking her to town to sell her," the woman answered him. "She's just one more cow than I need."

"How would you like to get rid of her right now so you wouldn't even have to go all the way to town to start with?" Jack asked. "How would you like to trade that cow for this horse and buggy?"

The woman could hardly believe it. She knew that the horse and buggy had to be worth three or four cows.

"You mean," she asked Jack, "that I could get the horse *and* the buggy for this one cow?"

"That's right," Jack answered her, "but you have to take *both* of them or it's no deal. You see, they're slowing me down from seeking my fortune." And so Jack traded the horse and the buggy for one milk cow.

Two days later Jack realized that he had made a big mistake. The old cow was dry, and he never got a single drop of milk from her. Besides that, she didn't like just eating grass along beside the road. No, the cow was always running off and getting into people's cornfields, and Jack spent half the time just getting her out of trouble. On top of that, the one time he tried to ride her, she threw him off and almost broke his neck.

"I've got to get shut of this old cow," Jack said. "I will never find my fortune as long as I keep having to chase after her." For the next day or two he stayed on the lookout for a way to get rid of the cow.

It was in the afternoon of the second day that Jack caught up with a young girl who was carrying a hen under her arm. She had helped a neighbor woman spring-clean her house, and the hen was what she had been paid for several days of work.

"Now, *that* is what I need," Jack said when he saw the hen. "Why, I could get eggs to eat every day, and it surely wouldn't take much food to feed one hen. I'll bet she would just follow me along and eat bugs anyway."

It didn't take much talking for the girl to agree to trade the hen for the cow. A cow was a lot better pay for house-cleaning than one hen ever could be. Jack thought he had made an easy deal for sure this time. He started down the road, still looking for his fortune, with the hen under his arm.

Before that one day was over, Jack knew that he was in a fix. He didn't even know that hen hadn't even laid an egg in over a year, but he did know that he had to carry her every step that he took. This would never do. He knew that he had to get rid of her.

While Jack had been doing all of this traveling and trading, he had hardly been able to get hold of a thing to eat. He sure was hungry.

"Maybe," he thought, "I can trade this hen in for some food. Then I won't starve to death while I'm looking for my fortune."

As soon as he came into a new town, that is exactly what he determined to do.

The first place where Jack saw any activity was the blacksmith shop. He walked inside with his hen under his arm, determined to trade her for something to eat.

The blacksmith was hammering on a horseshoe. When he stopped and looked up, Jack started in to his bargaining.

"Sir," he said to the blacksmith, "I am out seeking my fortune, but things keep getting in my way. Now, take this hen here. I don't really need her, and I wonder if I could trade her to you for something to eat?"

Jack did not know that this particular blacksmith was a man who was known far and wide to enjoy a good swap. And he was known as the one who always came out on top, no matter what was being traded.

He looked down at Jack and said, "Well, son, I could trade you some victuals for that hen, but that wouldn't be fair. Why, you'd eat that food up in no time, and then I'd still have your hen!

"What you need from me is something that would last. You need something that would feed you for a good long time. I'll tell you what, Jack," he said, "I'll trade you something that you can use to make just enough money each day so that you can buy food from now on. What do you think of that?"

Jack was awful pleased. He handed that hen right over to the blacksmith and waited to see what he was going to get in return for it.

The blacksmith took the old hen out the back door of his shop and put her under a tub where he could come back to wring her neck and cook her once he had got rid of Jack. Then he went out to the edge of his garden and scrounged up two good-sized yellow flint rocks.

He washed the rocks in the horse trough, then dried them and oiled them up until they were nice and shiny.

Jack was still waiting when the blacksmith came back in the shop door and dropped the two rocks down on the workbench in front of him. "Here you are, Jack!" he said.

Now, Jack thought that the yellow rocks were pretty, but he didn't have any idea about what they were for. Finally he asked the blacksmith, "How do I make money with these?"

"Oh, Jack," the blacksmith said, "I thought that you'd know. These here are nail-straightening rocks! You just put a bent nail on top of one of these rocks, hit it with the other, and the nail comes out straight. If you will just go from house to house, people will come out from everywhere with all of their crooked nails just waiting for you to straighten them out. Now, go to it Jack!"

Jack picked up the nail-straightening rocks and started out the door. He felt pretty good about his last trade because, even if he had never seen nail-straightening rocks before, he knew that he wouldn't have to feed them anything. He started down the road just looking for his first nail-straightening customers.

As Jack walked down the road, the first house he came to had a big covered well right out in the front yard. It was awful hot, and, as Jack headed up toward the house to see if they had any nails that needed straightening, he stopped by the well to draw him a drink of water.

He put his nail-straightening rocks down on the side of the well, dropped the bucket down the shaft; and, when he saw the rope straighten out, started to pull it up, hand over hand.

Jack had caught a good, full bucket of water, and it was a real chore to draw that rope up. He was really pulling.

Then, just as he got the bucket to the top, one of his elbows accidently hit the nail-straightening rocks and knocked both of them right down in the well. Jack heard them splash, and then they settled out of sight to the bottom.

He took a good, long drink of water. Then he stood up straight and smiled from ear to ear.

"I must be the luckiest man in the world!" Jack said, right out loud.

"I started out looking for my fortune, and for seven years I was held up by having a job. Then I was held up by having so much money I couldn't tote it, then a horse I had to feed, then a cow that ran off, then a hen that didn't lay eggs, then two rocks I had to carry—

"But now—now I can really go looking for my fortune because I don't have *one single thing* standing in my way to hold me up!"

And so Jack started off down the road again, still not knowing what a fortune was, but awfully happy to be looking for it!

The Time Jack
Told a Big Tale

Since this is a collection of stories told about Jack, it seemed good to include the one tale I remember hearing in which Jack himself is the storyteller. This was certainly one of my earliest favorites.

*T*here was one time when Jack and his mama were living in a little old shack of a house on a creekbank way down at the bottom of the same town where the king lived. Jack's daddy was already dead at this time, but Jack's brothers Tom and Will were still living there. Jack and the rest of them had got down to being so poor that about all they lived on was what they could grow themselves, and that was mostly cabbage and potatoes.

The king lived in a great big three-story house on the top of the biggest hill above this very same town. He owned the whole town and most of the countryside all around there. He was rich and had so much money that he would have needed some help if he wanted to spend it all.

Now, this old king was getting to be a right old man. He was fairly infirm and had to spend most of his days just wrapped up in the bed. He wasn't scared of dying because he had lived a good long life already, but he did get awful bored just wrapped up there in the bed day after day.

Besides being bored, there was one real thing in the world that was worrying the old king. That one thing was his daughter. The king had one daughter. She was about sixteen years old and was at least two-and-a-half times as pretty as anybody else in the whole country around there, *and* she was going to be the new queen someday because she was the only heir the king had.

The thing that was worrying the king was that he was afraid he might die before his daughter got married, and if that happened he would never have a chance to know who the next king would be. He wanted awful bad to know who was going to come after him before he died.

Now, back in those old days most of the poor people got married just because they loved one another, but the rich people didn't do it like that. No, the rich people always married whoever their daddies picked out for them. It worked out better than you would think, because doing it this way, the people getting married didn't know enough about one another to be disappointed once it was too late to get out of it.

So the old king decided that the thing for him to do was just to pick out somebody for his daughter to marry, and then he could rest easy because he would know for sure who the next king was going to be.

So he gathered up some of his chief wisemen and advisors, and all of them started talking about it.

"Who do you'all think my daughter ought to marry?" the king asked. Every one of those wisemen had a different answer.

One of them said, "She ought to marry the *handsomest* man in all the country, and that is that."

"What if he is the handsomest but turns out to be *stupid*?" the next one asked. "I think she ought to marry the *smartest* man—that's the one."

The third one of these advisors was ready. "Smart is all right, but what if he is *puny*? She really ought to marry the *strongest* man if he is going to be the new king."

The last of the wisemen was not to be outdone. "Strong bedads, I say! Why, the *strongest* man could *smell* like a hog pen. We can do better than that!"

The old king was fairly laughing by now, and it was the first time he had laughed in a good long while. "This is good," he said. "This is the most fun I've had in I don't know when. All four of you sure are some storytellers, and I do like that. Why, all this fun gives me an idea."

All the wisemen wanted to know what the king had thought of, and they waited for him to tell them.

"All of you know," he started, "that I spend most of the days wrapped up in bed, and that is awful boring. But we've had such a good time just now that I've figured out what to do.

"Let's just have every man in the kingdom who wants to marry my daughter come here and tell me a story. That way I will be entertained for days and days, and then I will pick one out to marry her."

So the word went out. The king was looking for somebody to marry his daughter and be the next king when he died. All you had to do to try out was go up there to the castle and *tell the king a story*. There wasn't anything to lose.

By now every man in the kingdom knew how pretty that girl was, *and* they knew how rich that old king was and what all he owned in land. So they started lining up at the castle door, all working on stories in their heads while they waited.

The old king had never had such a good time in all his life. He just laid there in bed and listened, day after day. He heard great adventure stories; he heard fortune-seeking stories; he heard about dreams; and he heard about demons. This was the best idea he had come up with in a long time. He forgot all about picking out somebody to marry his daughter.

After a few weeks some of the men had been there to tell stories a half-dozen times. They were wondering what you had to do to *win* this business. So they sent word in to the king to try to find out.

Well, the old king was having such a big time that he hadn't even thought about that. But he figured it was fair to let them know something or they wouldn't keep coming. So he got carried outside on his bed to where he could talk to them himself.

"Fellers," he said, "I sure do appreciate your trying to win my daughter, and those stories have been awful good. But to really win, somebody is going to have to tell me a story that is so fantastic that I just cannot possibly believe that it could ever be true. Yes, fellers, tell me a story that is beyond my imagination. If you can be the one to make me say, 'That's not true!', then you will be the winner right on the spot."

Now the stories really got wild. That old king heard things he had never imagined before. He liked what he was hearing so much that he would just lean back and close his eyes and say, "Oh, yes! That's good! I can just *see it now!*" And the stories went on and on.

After several months, the stories had just about run out. Even Jack's brothers Tom and Will had been up there two or three times each. Every man, old and young, had tried to win the contest with the king. Every one, that is, except old Jack.

Jack didn't think he knew any stories, and besides, he didn't have any clothes to wear up to the king's big house. So he had never really thought about trying.

One day Tom and Will started poking at him. "Jack," they said, "why don't you go on up there and tell the king a story? Everybody else in the whole countryside has tried and just about give out of ideas. You might be just the very one to hit on the right thing. We would like it awful well to be the new king's brothers."

"No," Jack said, "I better not. I don't know anything to tell, and besides, I don't have any good clothes to wear. I wouldn't know what to say if I did go up there."

"Aw, Jack," Tom said, "what you'd say will just come to you as you say it. And Will and I will fix you up to where you'll look real good. You're getting about big enough that I bet you could wear some of Daddy's old left-behind clothes. How about it?"

Jack thought it over and finally decided to give it a try.

Tom and Will spent all morning getting Jack all dressed up to go. He had to wear his own britches and shirt because even if he was pretty tall for his age, he still wasn't big enough around the middle to fill in his daddy's britches.

After that Tom picked out a long overcoat that their daddy used to wear and put that on Jack. It came just about clean to the ground. They put an old hat on Jack which did cover up all of his hair but also came down over his ears.

Finally Will said, "Now, Jack, a feller ought to have him a sword to wear to the king's house. We don't have a sword, but here is the blade off of a mowing scythe. Let's stick it through your belt and let it hang down, and it will maybe look a little bit like a sword where it pokes out of your coat at the bottom."

Jack was a sight to look at! There he went, dressed in that big, oversized coat and hat, on his way to the king's house, with his mowing-scythe sword sticking out at the bottom.

All the way through town Jack had people laughing and poking at the way he looked. But he didn't pay any attention to them. He was on his way to the king's house to tell a story—if he could come up with one.

At last Jack got up to that big old three-story house where the king lived. He walked right up onto the porch and knocked on the front door.

When the king's men opened the door, they fell right down on the floor laughing at Jack. He was about the funniest thing they had ever seen.

"Whoa, Jack!" one of them said, "you shore are a sight! What are you doing up here at the king's house, anyway?"

"I've come about the contest to be the new king," Jack told them, straightening up right tall. "I am planning to tell the king a story he will never believe. When he hears me he will say, *'Jack, that's not true!'* and I will get to marry his daughter."

Those men really rolled around and laughed when they heard this. It was about the most unbelievable thing *they* had heard for sure.

"So," said Jack, who was getting annoyed about all of this laughing by now, "take me in to see the king."

They took old Jack right up to the top floor of that three-story house and right on in to the king's bedroom. The old king was propped up in bed just waiting for whoever was coming to entertain him next. He wasn't expecting Jack, and when he saw him he laughed so hard that he about fell out of the bed!

"Jack!" he finally said, "it's you! I just about couldn't see you under that big coat and hat! What are you doing here?"

Jack was getting puckered up to pout by now. It seemed like everybody was laughing at him. He was wishing that he had not ever come, but he wasn't going to back out now.

"I have come to tell you a story that you will never believe," he said.

"That's a pretty good one, Jack," the king said. "You thought you were going to trick me right there from the start. You thought that I was going to say, *'That's not true'* as soon as you said that, didn't you? It's not going to work, Jack. So far, I believe everything you say."

Jack didn't even catch on to what the trick was supposed to be. The king was already way ahead of him.

The king smiled and went on, "Now, Jack. Tell me your story. Remember, now, that I know everything about you. Your daddy used to work for me when he was living. He was a good man, Jack. He used to raise forty acres of corn for me every year. He was a good, hard worker."

Jack was thinking hard and fast now. "He sure was," Jack replied to the king, "but he was not *half* the worker that I am. Did you know, King, that I raise *eighty* acres of corn all by myself every year, and I don't even have a mule to work it with? Do you believe that?"

"Of course I believe it, Jack," the king said. "I can just close my eyes right now and see you pulling that plow yourself. But tell me, Jack, do you cut all that corn and put it all up by yourself when it's ripe in the fall?"

"I do," said Jack. "How did you guess? I cut the entire eighty acres in one hour without the help of one single, living human being! Do you believe that?"

The king chuckled and answered, "I know that I do, Jack. I just can't quite get the picture of it in my head. How about telling me just a little bit more about how you do that, Jack, so I can get the picture."

"Sure," said Jack. "It started out like this. One day in the fall of the year I went out there to my big eighty-acre cornfield to cut a few stalks of corn for my cow. I had a little kitchen knife with me to do the cutting. About the time I got to the edge of the field, I saw a rabbit sitting there in the high grass, and I thought that I sure would like to have that rabbit to cook and eat for my supper.

"So," Jack went on, "I drew back that kitchen knife and threw it at that rabbit."

"I can see *that*, Jack," the king said. "Did you kill it?"

"Well, no. Just before the knife hit the rabbit, he turned around and *caught it in his mouth by the knife handle*. Then he took off running away with my kitchen knife.

"As that rabbit ran, he was hopping right along beside a row of corn, and, with that knife-blade sticking out of the side of his mouth, he was *cutting that whole row of corn right down!*

"When that rabbit got to the end of the row, I just clapped my hands to scare him, and he jumped around and started running down the next row. All I had to do was to clap once at the end of each row, and, in less than an hour, that rabbit cut all eighty acres of corn. Now, what do you think of that?"

"Oh, Jack. I can see it now!" the king said, with his eyes closed. "Look at that rabbit *go*! Did you eat him after that, Jack?"

"No," said Jack, "there wasn't enough to eat after that. He just wore himself out!"

The old king laughed and laughed. Jack thought to himself, "This king will believe *anything*! I'll never get him to say, 'That's not true,' no matter what I tell him. No wonder his daughter's not married yet. I might as well give up now and go on back home."

The king had a different idea, though. "Tell me another one, Jack. That rabbit business was good! Tell me another one."

"You want to hear another story, do you?" Jack asked the king. "This time I *will* tell you one you will never believe."

Jack thought to himself for a few minutes, and then he started.

"Do you remember, King, a few years ago when we had that bad drought? When it didn't rain for about four months and all of the corn just about dried up? Do you remember that?"

"Of course I do," the king said. "Why, if we hadn't had some corn brought in from over in England, a lot of people would have starved to death!"

"That's right," Jack went on. "I was just a little old boy back then, but *I* am the very one who went over to England and brought back that very load of corn that saved everybody! Do you believe that?"

"If you say it's true, Jack, I know I believe you," the king answered. "But you're going to have to go on and tell me a little more about how you actually did it."

Jack wound up and started. "It was like this," he said. "I came from my house all the way up through town until I was almost right up here to where you live. I wanted to get a good running start downhill, you see.

"Well, sir, I ran downhill from here about halfway through town; and when I was going as fast as I could, I jumped. I mean, I *jumped* so high and so far that I sailed all the way over the ocean and landed right there in England. Do you believe that?"

"I can see it now, Jack! What a jump. I can just see you flying through the clouds across the big water. Go on, Jack!"

Jack thought, "He *will* believe anything!" but he kept on talking just the same.

"When I landed in England, it made such a big noise that the king's men over there came out to see what it was. When they saw who it was, they said, 'Law, Jack! What do you want?'

"I told them that we was having a drought and that I needed to take five hundred bushels of corn back to save our people. They took me in to see their king, and he told them to set me up with the five hundred bushels right on the spot."

"How did you get back with it?" the king asked Jack.

"I'm coming to that part if you'll just wait." Jack was thinking about as hard and fast as he could.

"They asked me if I had anything to carry the corn in. At first I started to say 'no,' but just about then I felt something biting me on the back of the neck. I slapped at it and found out it was a flea. So I picked up that flea and said to the king's men, 'Just you let me borrow a knife to skin this flea with, and I will make a flea-skin sack out of its hide that I can carry my corn in.'"

Jack didn't dare stop talking. He was really on a roll now.

"I skinned that flea and turned its hide inside out, and it made a mighty fine sack for carrying corn. Of course, the hard part was getting the first little bit of corn into it. But after I got that flea-skin started to stretching, why, it just got bigger and I could load it a bushel at a time.

"Well, King, would you believe I finally loaded five hundred bushels of corn into that sack I made from the skin of just one flea?"

"I can see it now," the king said. "What a sack. I truly can see it getting bigger and bigger in my mind's eye. What a load of corn! How did you get back home with it, Jack? Did that corn-cutting rabbit help you out this time?" The king was grinning when he said it, but Jack didn't pay any attention to him.

"I'm coming to that part, too." Jack's mind really was moving fast now.

"At first I thought about jumping back just like I had jumped over there to start with," he kept going on, "but then I realized that with the big load of corn I might not make it all the way across. So I sat down to figure out another way to do it.

"While I was sitting there, a whole huge flock of wild geese came over and then landed right in the edge of the cornfield. That gave me an idea. I asked the king's men if they could get me two good, long pieces of stout cord. Then I took those cords and tied one to the left foot and the other one to the right foot of every single one of those geese. There must have been a thousand of them. When I got finished, I had me a string of geese half a mile long, each one about a foot behind the next one.

"All I had to do then," Jack said, "was to tie the ends of those cords to myself and my flea-skin bag. Then when those geese decided to take off to flying, they carried us right up into the air. Those two cords were just like reins on those geese. I could guide them by pulling either on their left feet or their right ones. I guided them right over the ocean until we were right here and back at home!"

"I can see it now, "the king said. "That was a beautiful sight in my head to see that great string of geese hauling you and your corn-sack back over the ocean. That was a good story, Jack, but I am afraid that I *do* believe every word of it. Why don't you come back and try to tell me another one again another day?"

"Not so fast," Jack said. "This story's not over yet. The geese haven't landed yet. In fact, that part turned out to be the biggest problem of the whole trip.

"When we got back close to here, I discovered that even if I could make those geese turn left and right, I couldn't figure out how to make them land. We circled right around here above your very house five or six times, and those geese just got higher and higher."

"What did you do, Jack?" the king asked.

"Well," Jack went on, "I finally decided that I was just going to have to let loose and fall on down to the ground. I tried to guide those geese around over the edge of town, and when we got over there I cut the corn loose. Then I circled them around those big, soft pine trees above town, and that's where I let loose.

"I was coming down just fine," Jack said, "until a big puff of wind caught me. That wind blew me off track, and instead of landing in those soft pine trees, I landed feet first on that great big flat granite rock that is right up there above town."

The king wasn't saying a word now, but he sure was listening hard.

"When I hit that rock"—Jack was not even slowing down now—"I was falling so fast that I sank into the rock itself right up to my neck, just like sinking in mud! I couldn't move anything but my head, and I didn't know how I would ever get out. I kept thinking that I had to get word to Mama so she could come up there and pull me out of that rock.

"Then," Jack went on, "I got an idea. My sword here (Jack patted the mowing-scythe blade as he talked) had landed on the rock right beside my head, and when I saw it, I knew what to do.

"I reached out with my chin, got my sword under the edge, and pulled it right up against my neck. Then I started rubbing my neck back and forth on the blade so I could cut my head off."

The king's eyes were getting bigger and bigger as he listened.

"Yes, sir," Jack smiled, "I kept sawing away until I cut my own head off. My head rolled right down off of that rock and landed in the road. I hollered, 'Head for home!' and my head started rolling down the road to get Mama.

"Everything was going just fine until, about halfway home, my head rolled past a den where an old fox lived. It was a fox that was already mad at me because I had chased him out of the henhouse a few times before now. And when my head rolled by, that fox started chasing it!

"Boy, was that some race! My head was just rolling and bouncing along as hard and fast as it could with my hair and ears and tongue all a-flopping, but that fox was coming faster and faster and gaining with every step. It looked for sure like that fox was going to have my head! But then, I got an idea.

"All of a sudden I stopped my head, right there in the road, and just stared at that fox. This surprised him so much that he stopped for a minute right there. And when he did, I said to him, *'You come one step closer and I will stomp you to death!'* And do you know what? That old fox got so scared that he tucked his tail between his legs and ran back toward where he had come from!"

"What a stupid fox!" the king laughed out loud.

"Not half as stupid as you are!" Jack said, looking straight at the king.

"THAT'S NOT TRUE!" The king fairly shouted…and…then he realized what he had said. Jack *had* told the king a story that he couldn't believe!

And that is how Jack came to marry the king's daughter. Some people say that he became the next king, too. But other people say that Jack decided to give that job to someone else, because he didn't want to have to waste all of his time having to tell other people what to do.

The Time Jack
Got His First Job

Even though my intention is to include a number of Jack tales different from those in the standard collections, it may be of value to offer one very common story for comparing with other widely-known versions. I know of no more common tale than this one.

O ne time Jack and his mama were living all by themselves in a little house that was a good way on out from town. Tom and Will were living there, too; and, as usual, all of them put together were still just as poor as they could be. Tom and Will tried to help out with things the best they knew how, but at this time Jack was a little old half-grown boy who wasn't worth much as far as helping out was concerned.

Jack's mama always called him "my baby," and he really didn't know how to do much of anything. Why, he never did learn how to make up beds or wash dishes or pick up his clothes. He couldn't cook or iron or chop wood or even feed chickens and gather the eggs. He couldn't even milk the cow! That was all because he was his mama's "baby."

One day Jack came to his mama and said, "Mama, I need to get a job so I can make some money."

Jack had never actually seen any money in his life. He had heard about what money was and what it was good for, but his mama was so poor that there had not been one cent of money in their house since Jack got old enough to know what money was.

"Oh, Jack," his mama said, "you know that *I* don't have any money to give you. If I did, I'd give you a job working right here around the house. But I can't, because I don't have any money."

"I know about that, Mama," Jack said. "I was just thinking that I would go to town and get me a real job there!"

Jack's mama laughed. "Oh, Jack, you can't do that," she said. "Jack, my baby, you don't know how to do *anything*. How in the world are you going to get a job?"

"I don't know, Mama, "Jack pouted, "but I am going to do it. I just have to find some way to get some money."

And so Jack started on his way into town to try to find a job for himself.

He went from one store to the next. A lot of them had signs in the windows that said "HELP WANTED," but every time Jack went inside a store it was the same old thing.

"I'm looking for a job," he would say.

"What can you do?" the store owner would ask him.

"*Nothing!*" Jack would answer.

He went all the way through town and never did manage to get a job. He was awful discouraged by this and started to walk on back home when he got an idea. "I'm going to try one more time," Jack said to himself. "But this time I think I know what I'm doing."

So Jack stopped at the first farm house he came to and walked right up to the door and knocked. The farmer opened the door and just looked down at Jack.

"Hello, son," he said. What can I do for you?"

"I'm looking for a job," said Jack. "Do you need any help around here?"

"Around here," the farmer answered, "we *always* need help. What can you do?"

This time Jack said, *"Anything!"*

The farmer smiled and said, "Come on in, Jack...you're hired! How much do you want to get paid?"

Jack didn't have any idea about this, so he just told the farmer to pay him whatever he thought was right.

The farmer smiled to himself, and they went to work right on the spot. It was the fall of the year, and the farmer and Jack spent the whole day raking up leaves and pine needles. They picked up sticks all around the farmer's yard and cleaned out all the gutters on the house. At the end of the day, Jack was worn out, but he was anxious to come back to work on the next day because he had a real job.

Just as Jack started to leave to go home, the farmer said, "Wait a minute, Jack. You have to get paid."

Jack was amazed. "You mean I get paid after working just one day?" he asked. "I thought people had to work a week or so before they could get paid."

"No," said the farmer. "Around here people get paid every day. That's what I believe in." And for working *all day long,* the farmer gave Jack a quarter!

Now, old Jack didn't even know that this wasn't a lot of money. All he knew was that this was the first piece of money he had ever touched in his life...and...it was his!

He started home with the quarter in his hand. "Money!" he said to himself. "Real money! I'm going to be rich! I'm going to be rich!" Jack was so happy that he was throwing the quarter up in the air and then catching it as it came back down.

He kept on doing this as he walked along home. When he was almost there, he came to a place where he had to cross a footlog over a little creek. As he crossed the log, he tossed the quarter up into the air, but he missed it as it came down and the coin fell in the water and washed away.

"Oh, well," thought Jack. "It's a good thing I'm going back to work tomorrow. I'll get paid again then."

When Jack got home his mama was curious about where he had been all day. "You must have found a job, Jack," she said. "Tell me all about it."

So Jack told about his job at the farmer's house and about getting paid at the end of the first day.

"That's good, Jack," his mama said. "Let me see your money."

Then Jack had to tell about throwing the money up in the air and dropping it in the creek.

"Jack!" said his mama, who just couldn't believe what she was hearing. "Jack, what good does it do you to get a job and work if you're just going to drop your pay in the creek?

"When you go back to work tomorrow, Jack, I'll tell you what to do. You take your pay and *put it straight in your pocket,* and don't you take it out until you get home. Don't throw it up in the air, Jack!"

"All right, Mama," Jack said.

The next day, Jack went back to work at the farmer's house. On the way he happened to pass the king's house. It was the biggest house Jack had ever seen. It was three stories high and had porches running all around all three stories where you could come out and look over the countryside.

Jack thought out loud, "One of these days I am going to have a house like this. But at a quarter a day, it may take me a year or two before I can save up for it."

That day at the farmer's house Jack helped him clean out the barn where the cows stayed. It was a nasty job, and it took a long time, since Jack tried to hold his nose with one hand and shovel with the other.

When the barn was all cleaned out, they put in a new layer of clean sawdust to soak up the mud and to give the cows something to sleep on in the wintertime.

At the end of the day, when it was time to go home, Jack stuck out his hand to get his pay.

After all of that cow business, instead of a quarter, the farmer gave Jack a full bucket of milk.

Jack started home with the milk, then remembered what his mama had said: "Don't throw your pay up in the air, Jack. Put it straight in your pocket."

It was hard for Jack to get the milk in his pocket. First, he twisted his pants around until the pocket was almost on the front. Then he started pouring.

The pocket would fill up, but, if Jack waited a minute, the milk would go down and then he could pour in some more! Jack walked home with milk squishing in his shoes.

When his mama saw him she was excited. "Jack," she said, "did you get home with your pay today? What did you get? Another quarter?"

"You'll never guess what I got, Mama...a whole bucket of milk! And it is right here in my pocket!" Jack reached into his pocket and discovered that the milk was not there!

His mama couldn't believe it. "Jack, why did you pour milk into your pocket?"

"You told me to, Mama. You said, 'Don't throw it in the air. Put it in your pocket.'"

"I was talking about *money,* Jack, not milk. Are you going to work tomorrow?"

"Yes," Jack answered.

"If you get *money,* it goes in your pocket, Jack. But anything else will already be in what you're supposed to carry it in. Don't pour milk out of what it's in, Jack. Leave it in whatever he puts it in. Have you got that?"

"Yes, Mama," Jack whined. The next day he headed on back to the farmer's house.

This was the day for butter-churning at the farmer's house. After Jack helped out with a few odd chores, he fell into helping the farmer and his wife with the butter-making.

The farmer's wife had saved two big crocks of cream from the milk of the cows. Jack helped to carry the cream from the spring house and pour it into the big wooden churn. He did most of the churning to help her. There was so much cream that it filled the churn up twice.

When Jack finished the first churning, the farmer's wife worked up the butter while Jack churned the second churnful of cream.

As the farmer's wife worked up the butter, she put it into stone crocks, and the farmer put the crocks into the cold water in the springhouse to keep the butter cool.

At the end of the day, Jack got ready to go home. For his pay, the farmer's wife had saved out one big last ball of fresh butter. It must have weighed two pounds!

She said to Jack, "Give me your hat, Jack." Then she took Jack's hat, lined it with grape leaves, put the butter in it, and covered it with more grape leaves to shade the butter from the sun. She handed the hat back to Jack.

"Now, you run home, Jack. Hurry as fast as you can so the butter won't melt," she told him.

Jack started running, but it was hard to run carrying that hat with both hands. "I know what," he thought. Jack put his hat right on his head with the butter inside. Now he could run better and could swing his arms as he moved along.

It was a hot day, and as Jack ran the butter melted. It ran down around his ears and down his face and down through his hair until, by the time Jack got home, he was buttered all the way to the ground!

His mama took one look at him and said, "Jack! You are a mess. Why, if I had a great big biscuit I would just roll you around in it so I could get some of that butter back. Now, why did you do that?"

"Well, Mama," Jack explained, *"they* put it in my hat, and *you* told me to leave it in what they put it in. That's exactly what I did!"

"But Jack," his mama said, not knowing whether to laugh or cry, "you were supposed to carry your hat in your *hands,* not on your head!"

"That wouldn't have worked, Mama. As hot as it was today, that butter would have melted anyway. You know it would have got soft, and then it would have run right out of my hands."

"Now, Jack," replied his mama, thinking carefully about what she was about to say, "how do you keep butter cold? You know…you put it down in the cold water. Right? That's why we have a springhouse."

"Of course that's right, Mama," he answered.

"You, Jack, you walk all the way home right along beside the creek. If that butter gets soft, all you have to do is dip it in the cold water and cool it back off again. Can you remember that until tomorrow if you need to?"

"I'll try to remember that, Mama," he said.

The next day, bright and early, Jack was on his way back to the farmer's house.

All that day Jack helped the farmer and his wife mow hay. They mowed and raked and piled up hay until Jack knew they surely had enough to last all winter.

At the end of the day Jack was just sure that the farmer was going to give him a pile of hay for his pay. Instead, the farmer looked at Jack and said, "Today, Jack I am going to give you something that you will really like. It's old enough to take it from its mother."

Then the farmer disappeared into the barn and in a few minutes came back out with a small puppy.

Jack was thrilled! He took the puppy and thought to himself, "Don't throw it in the air … don't put it in your pocket …

don't carry it under your hat..." He started home carrying the puppy in his hands.

Before he had gone very far, Jack began to notice that the puppy was very *warm*. He also noticed that the puppy was awfully *soft*. Soon the puppy was wiggling so much that Jack thought, "This puppy is trying to run out of my hands!"

Then he remembered what his mama had told him to do. So he took the puppy down to the creek and dipped it in the cold water.

Jack started on home, but pretty soon that puppy was soft and wiggly again, so it was back in the water for another cooling off.

By the time Jack got all the way home, the puppy had had six baths and was blowing bubbles out of its nose!

"Jack!" his mama cried, "what are you doing? Did you try to drown your pay?"

"No, Mama," he answered her. "I was just doing what you told me to do. I carried the puppy in my hands, and when it got soft like it was going to run out of my hands, I cooled it off in the creek the way you told me to!"

"I was talking about butter, Jack, not puppies," his mama said. "Do you know how to bring puppies home?"

Jack's mama went in to the kitchen and came back out with a piece of heavy cord. She held the cord out to Jack and said, "Look at this, Jack. Put this in your pocket, and if that farmer gives you anything else that is like this puppy, you tie this cord around its neck, then lead it home on the end of this string. Do you have that?"

"I'll remember, Mama. I always do what you tell me."

The next day Jack helped the farmer and his wife make apple cider. They gathered up all of the apples that had fallen on the ground under the trees. Then they cut them up, and Jack and the farmer squeezed them in the apple press while the farmer's wife gathered up the jugs she had saved to put the cider in.

These were big glass jugs that would hold about a gallon each. They had a neck with a glass ring to put your finger through to carry them and small lids that screwed onto the top of the neck. Jack and the farmer and the farmer's wife worked all day. They would put a big funnel into the neck of the empty jug so they wouldn't spill any cider while they poured it. By the end of the day, the three of them had filled and capped nearly twenty gallons of apple cider.

Jack got ready to get his pay and go home. Sure enough, for working all of this day, the farmer gave Jack a gallon of cider.

Jack looked at the jug and thought, "Don't throw it up in the air...don't pour it in your pocket...don't carry it in your hat...don't throw it in the creek..."

About that time Jack noticed that the apple cider jug did in fact have a *neck*! And he remembered that he had that cord that his mama had given him right there in his pocket.

So Jack took out the cord, tied it around the neck of the jug, and started leading the jug of apple cider home behind him.

The road was filled with rocks, and along the way the jug broke on one and all the cider ran out. When Jack got home, he was just dragging the string.

His mama saw him and scratched her head. "What kind of dog did you start with, Jack?"

"Apple cider!" Jack replied, and then told his mother everything that had happened to him on that day.

This time Jack's mama really didn't know what to say or do. "I give up, Jack!" she nearly cried. "I just give up! I don't know what to tell you after this. Are you really going back to work tomorrow?"

"Yes, Mama," he answered. "If I go back tomorrow, I'll have a whole week of work behind me."

Jack's mama didn't say anything else at the time. She just couldn't think of what to say. She and Jack ate their supper while she thought and thought about how to send him off on the following day. When it was almost time to go to bed, Jack's mama reached down into a drawer of the cupboard and took out a great big empty flour sack. She unfolded the big sack and held it up in front of Jack.

"Now, Jack," she started, "I just don't have any idea what that farmer might give you for your pay today. But I'll tell you what … whatever it is, just put it in this sack, and then carry it home on your back! You got that, Jack?"

"Yes, Mama." He took the sack. "Put it in this sack, and then carry it home on my back. I'll not forget, Mama."

And so the next day, Jack started back to the farmer's house with the empty flour sack slung over his shoulder.

On the way there, he again passed the king's house. While he was looking up at the king's big house and admiring it, Jack saw the king's daughter looking out the window. She was beautiful, but she also was crying.

She was always crying. Her mother had died two years before that, and she had started crying and never stopped.

Jack remembered what the king had told everybody. If anybody could get her to stop crying, he would give them *two wagonloads of gold*. Jack thought, "If I were smart enough, I would do that and I wouldn't have to go to work anymore. But I'm just not that smart, so I'll just have to keep on working."

On he went to work at the farmer's house.

On this day Jack and the farmer were cutting wood for the winter. They would saw a big log up into short lengths and then split them. It took a lot of firewood to get through the winter. They worked all day long.

At the end of the day, the time came for Jack to get paid. "Jack," the farmer said, "you have been working for me for a whole week. I want to give you something special today. Why, this is something that could even help you get home…if you work it right."

Then the farmer disappeared into the barn and in a few minutes came back out with a *donkey!*

Jack couldn't believe it. Why, this was something he had always wanted, and it was his. All he had to do was to figure out how to get home with it.

He remembered everything he had learned all week. He could hear the voice of his mama: "Don't throw it up in the air...don't put it in your pocket...don't carry it in your hat...don't dip it in the creek..." The donkey did have a neck, but Jack didn't have the piece of cord with him today that he had pulled the cider home with the day before.

Then he remembered that his mama had given him something to help him out. It was the sack.

"Now, what did Mama say?" Jack tried hard to remember. "'Put it in the sack.'"

He tried to put the donkey into the sack by starting with its tail. That didn't work. Then he tried with each of its feet. No luck there either.

Finally Jack folded the donkey's ears back and put the sack as far as it would go down over the donkey's head. The donkey hated it! It didn't like having its ears folded back to start with. Besides that, the donkey couldn't see and couldn't half breath. It was dancing around, slinging its head back and forth and "hee-hawing" for all it was worth!

"Whoa," Jack was talking out loud, mostly to himself. "I reckon I've got it about as far in the sack as it will go. All I've got to do now is to figure out how to get it on my back."

Jack tried to pick the donkey up every way he could think of. Finally he got down on the ground and crawled right under the donkey. He stuck his head between the donkey's front legs and then wrapped one of his arms around each of those same front legs. When he had a good grip, Jack stood up.

It was an awful load! The front of the donkey was now on Jack's back. The donkey's head, still covered with the sack, stuck up over Jack's head, while the donkey's back feet were still trying to keep their balance on the ground.

With Jack huffing and puffing and with the donkey "hee-hawing" and staggering all over the place with its hind feet, the two of them started making their way along the road from the farmer's house back toward where Jack lived.

"We'll never get home...we'll never get home..." Jack said out loud over and over again as he carried the front of the donkey.

"We'll never get anywhere...hee-haw...we'll never get anywhere!" is what the donkey was thinking at the same time.

All of a sudden Jack heard a door slam.

He looked up at the noise, and there stood the king, right there in the middle of the road.

"Jack!" the king spoke. He was excited about something for sure. "Jack...*you must be the smartest boy in the world!*

"Why, my daughter has not only stopped crying, she is rolling over and over on the floor, laughing her own silly head right off! She told me that she looked out the window and saw a blindfolded singing donkey riding up the road on the back of a boy. How did you ever think of that?

"Come on in, Jack. You get *two* wagonloads of gold."

And so Jack went in to the king's house, and the king gave him two wagonloads of gold, plus the horses and wagons to get it home.

The king also took the sack off of the donkey's head so that the donkey could follow along to Jack's house, too.

When Jack got home to his mama, he had so much gold that he never had to go back to work again.

The Time Jack
Fooled the Miller

One of the first times I became aware that I had learned some stories which were not known by all children came when, as an undergraduate English student, I discovered that I already knew Chaucer's "Reeve's Tale" before I ever read it. Of course, the story as I knew it was about Jack, but the plot trick was exactly the same. Here is that wonderful "adult" story about one of Jack's best tricks.

One time Jack and his mama and his brothers Tom and Will were living way off in the mountains outside of town. They tried to raise their own food and also did a little bit of hunting just to try to put meat on the table.

There weren't many real close neighbors around there, but about two miles from their house there did live a miller who always ground their corn for them when they needed some cornmeal. The miller was an old man who lived up in the loft over his mill. He was known far and wide as a braggart and a trickster.

Not only did the old miller actually pull a lot of trickery on people, his favorite pastime was bragging and telling everybody about how smart he was and all the tricks he had pulled.

"Why, I could steal the bedsheets off of a bed while you are asleep and you'd never know it ... I could steal the food off of your knife while it's between your plate and your mouth ... I could steal *anything* right under your nose ..." This was all the old man talked about.

People around there knew that what the miller said was partly true. He was a trickster. Part of the proof was that while he was past sixty years old, he had a wife who was only sixteen and a new baby less than a year old. Everybody thought that was a good trick right in itself for a man as old as he was. Still, people did get awful tired of having to listen to him brag all the time.

"Old man," some of the neighbors would say, "one of these days somebody is going to steal something from you. Then you'll be sorry that you did all of this bragging."

"That will never happen," the miller vowed and declared. "Nobody will *ever* steal anything off of me. Why, if anybody was ever to steal just one thing off of me, or if anybody could just come to do business at the mill without my stealing something off of them while they were there, why, *I'd give them the deed to this mill and everything that I own right along with it!*"

When what the miller had said got spread around the community, everybody living around there took it as a challenge to try to make a fool out of him. But it seemed that the harder people tried, the more the miller was able to steal from them. They were off their own guard when they were trying to pull something on him.

It wasn't long until everybody around there had tried, failed, and given up. The only people who hadn't given it a try were Tom and Will and Jack.

They had talked about it often enough, but every time they were working on a good plan, somebody else would try it and would fail. Jack kept saying that it just wasn't worth wasting your time to try. He said that they just ought to give up and go on about their own business.

Then one day Tom came up with a new idea. "Let's go at him two on one," he said. "Let's go up there to get some corn ground, and while one of us watches the corn go in at the top of the mill, the other one can watch the cornmeal come out at the bottom. That way he can't possibly steal anything from us, *and* maybe one of us can pick up something of his while he's not looking."

"That's a good plan," Will said. "I'll go for it with you."

Jack shook his head. "You two go on. I just don't want anything to do with that old man. He's too slick for me."

And so Tom and Will got ready. They shelled out about a half-bushel of corn, sacked it up, and both of them rode double-bareback on their daddy's horse to the miller's house.

Once there, they tied the horse to a tree in the yard, then carried the sack of corn inside to get on with their plan.

The miller took the sack of corn. Tom stationed himself at the bottom of the chute and held an empty sack to catch the ground cornmeal. He was going to watch to see that the miller didn't steal even a grain of his cornmeal.

Will followed the miller up to the hopper where he poured the corn in the top of the mill to be ground. He was making sure that not a single grain of corn ended up in the miller's pocket.

The miller opened the watergate to start the mill to grinding while Tom and Will had their eyes glued to what they thought was happening.

The miller noticed how hard Tom and Will were concentrating on the corn-grinding, and he knew that they couldn't be paying attention to anything else while this was going on. So he slowed down the water so the mill would take a lot longer to grind the corn, then slipped out the door into the yard and left Tom and Will watching inside.

Once in the yard, the miller noticed their horse tied to the tree. He walked over and asked out loud, "Does this horse belong to anybody around here?"

Of course Tom and Will couldn't hear him from inside the running mill. The miller then said, "All right, since nobody claims this horse, I guess he must belong to me."

He untied the horse and put it in the barn up above the mill.

When the miller got back to the mill, the corn was just finishing up and the last grains of meal were falling into Tom's sack. Tom tied the sack up tight, and then said to the miller, "Well, we did it! We ground a whole half-bushel of corn, and you didn't steal even one grain from us!"

"You boys sure are smart, all right," the miller smiled at them. "Go on home, and this afternoon I'll bring you the deed to the mill."

Tom and Will laughed out loud to one another as they went out the door of the mill. Then they looked up and saw that their daddy's horse was gone.

"Have you seen our horse?" Will asked the miller.

The miller said, "Well, *I* have a new horse that somebody left out here for me. I asked all around to see whether it belonged to anyone else, but nobody spoke up. And since it was trespassing on my land, I took it to be meant for me!"

With that, Tom and Will found out that they hadn't won after all. They had to walk all the way home, carry their own cornmeal, *and* tell their mama and Jack what had happened to their horse. It was terrible!

Jack said, "I told you not to mess with him. The harder you try, the trickier he gets. I am not going to mess around with that old man at all."

A few weeks after that, Jack decided to go off hunting for the day. He got his daddy's old muzzle-loading gun, a powder-horn full of gunpowder, and some home-made bullets. Then he started off through the woods.

He didn't have any luck at all close to home that day, so he walked farther and farther, determined to find something to shoot for supper. By the late afternoon Jack had still not had any good luck at all, and so he started walking back home.

It was completely dark long before Jack got even halfway back. He knew from the kind of night it was that he was sure to have a terrible time finding his way home. It was pitch dark and so cloudy that you couldn't even see the stars. There wasn't any moon, and, of course, way out there in the country there were no lights of any kind to be seen. It hadn't even occurred to Jack that he might have needed to carry a lantern with him on a hunting trip like this.

Jack was tripping over roots and rocks; he was running smack into trees; he was stumbling into creeks. It was so dark out there that Jack had to reach up with his fingers and feel to see whether his eyes were open or shut!

All of a sudden Jack ran smack into the side of a building. He felt his way along the wall in the dark, and when he came to the mill wheel he realized that he had stumbled into the mill where that tricky miller lived with his wife and baby.

"Maybe," Jack thought, "maybe the miller will let me spend the night here, and then I can go on home tomorrow morning in the daylight."

So Jack felt his way back around the mill until he came to the door. There he knocked and waited to see if anyone was inside.

Nobody came to the door, and Jack realized that there was no light burning in the house and that maybe nobody was at home. He knocked one more time and heard somebody stirring around way on the inside.

Finally the door opened, and there he saw the miller standing in the dark. He was wearing his nightshirt, and it looked to Jack like he had been asleep for a while.

"Why, Jack," the miller said, "what are you doing knocking around here so late at night? Don't you know that I have a young wife and that she needs to go to bed early?"

"It's not all that late," Jack said. "I'll bet it's not past eight o'clock. It's just so dark at this time of year that you think it's late."

"Well, anyway, Jack, what can I do for you?"

"I got stuck out here and it got dark on me. I wonder if you might have space for me to spend the night, and then I could go on home tomorrow morning in the light of day."

"Why, sure, Jack," the miller said. "We've got plenty of beds. You know that the miller who lived here before I came had a big family, and he left me a houseful of beds. Come on in … there's plenty of room."

Jack started to step in the door, and then the miller said, "Wait a minute, Jack. You better go visit the outhouse before we go in. I don't keep any bed pots in the house, and you might need to go before morning."

So Jack went to the outhouse and then followed the miller inside the mill.

It was so dark that the miller lighted a candle to see the way. They went up the stairs to the loft, following the light of the one candle.

Once there, Jack looked around the big room. There was a fireplace at one end, but, since it was a warm night, the fire had all burned out. There were six big double beds arranged around the walls of the loft room. In one of them the miller's wife was sound asleep. Her baby was sleeping in a cradle on the floor beside that bed.

The miller turned to Jack and said, "Take your choice, Jack. Any bed you want is yours. My wife and I sleep in all of them at one time or another. We usually sleep in one until it gets dirty, and then we move on to the next. That way it takes about a year before they all get dirty enough for us to have to wash all the sheets at once."

Jack picked out a bed on the opposite wall, as far as he could get from the miller and his wife. He undressed and crawled into bed while the miller blew out the candle and crawled into his own bed with his young wife.

Jack was almost asleep when suddenly an idea hit him.

"It sure is dark," he thought, "and it sure is early. And with no pots under any of the beds, I'll bet that the miller's wife will never make it through the night without having to go to the outhouse. I think I'll just stay awake right here for a while to see what happens."

Jack propped himself up in bed in the dark. He couldn't see a thing, but he could hear every move made in that room, even the sound of breathing as the miller and his wife and baby were sound asleep.

It was not actually very long until Jack heard the sound of breathing change and then heard the covers rustle across the room. Then he heard the sound of a pair of little feet hit the floor. He could hear the miller's wife feel her way around the room until she found the top of the stairs. He could hear her whisper to herself about how dark it was. He could hear her make her way down the steep stairs, and he could hear the mill door close as she went outside for her late-night visit to the outhouse.

As soon as he was sure she was outside, Jack slipped out of his bed. He eased over to the bed where the miller was asleep, picked up the cradle with the sleeping baby in it, carried it across the room, and put the baby cradle back down *right beside the bed where he, Jack, was sleeping.*

Once back in his own bed, Jack started listening again.

He heard the downstairs door open and shut as the miller's wife felt her way back inside the darkened mill.

Jack heard her feeling her way slowly back up the stairs to the loft. When she got to the top of the stairs, he heard her talking out loud to herself about how dark it was. "Now, where *is* my bed?" she said. "It is so dark in here that you can't see the end of your nose!"

She felt her way around the room to where she thought her bed was, but when she felt to see whether her baby was covered up, the cradle was not there.

"I must be turned around," she said to herself. "We keep switching beds so much that I can't remember where I was sleeping."

Jack listened as she felt her way on around the room, feeling from bed to bed, trying to find the one where the baby cradle was. When she found it, she was standing right beside Jack. She covered the baby back up, gave the cradle a little rock, and, thinking she had now come to the right bed, climbed right up in there with old Jack!

Nobody knows if or when she found out she was in the wrong bed. But whether she did or not, she stayed right there for the rest of the night.

Jack slept pretty late into the next morning. After all, he had stayed up later than he usually did. When he opened his eyes at last, the first thing he saw was the miller sitting at a table writing on a sheet of paper. The old miller had already signed the mill over to Jack, and he was writing out a deed to turn the rest of what he owned into Jack's name as well!

"Jack," the miller said, "you did it ... you are the first person in this world to ever steal anything from me! I keep my word. You win!"

So Jack moved right into the mill that was now his. The miller did get to keep his wife and baby even though Jack could have said that they were part of the deal, too.

People say that Jack ran that mill for a good long time before he gave it to his brothers so he could go out on the road again to seek his fortune.

The Time Jack
Cured the Doctor

This is one of those tales about Jack which seemed more like a joke I wasn't supposed to hear than an actual story. It was of the type generally passed around the community and repeated by many people, especially by adolescent boys or even older men on camping or hunting trips. It was in the latter setting that I first remember overhearing it when I was supposed to be asleep.

One time, after Jack was mostly grown up, he and his mama and brothers Tom and Will were living out in the country not too far from where an old country doctor lived.

This old doctor and his wife lived in a fairly nice frame house up on the top of a big hill. Besides the doctor and his wife, they had one daughter living with them.

One daughter was enough, because this girl was pretty well grown up, and she had turned so pretty while she was growing up that all of the men and boys in the whole countryside would stand in line just to get a good look at her.

She was such a looker that simply gazing at her would curl a young man's hair and make an old man pass right out cold on the ground.

The bad part about all this was that all this beauty was keeping the old doctor and his wife from being able to get any sleep. All night long there would be old boys whistling from the yard, chunking little rocks on top of the house, and even pecking on the windows, trying to get that girl to come out of the house so they could court her for a little while.

After a time, the old doctor and his wife got real tired of this, and he decided on a plan.

"We're never going to get any peace and quiet," he told his wife, "until that girl is just married off and gone. Let's go ahead and get her married off and out of here so we can settle down and get us some rest again." She agreed.

Now, this was in the old times when daddies still got to pick out the men that their daughters were going to marry, so the first thing the old doctor had to do was to decide on what kind of a man he wanted his daughter to get married to. He thought and thought about it and even talked it over with his own wife. After all, they didn't want her getting married off just to have her come back home in a week or two. They wanted her gone for good, so they both wanted to pick out a man who would last.

The doctor's wife was the one who finally came up with the idea. She said to her husband, "You have made a pretty good life out of being a doctor. Why don't you get our girl married off to a doctor? That way she'd be well taken care of!"

"That's a fine idea," the old doctor said. "Only trouble is that I'm the only doctor around here. That leaves it so there's nobody to marry her off to."

"Well, then," said his wife, "why don't we marry her off to somebody who wants to be a doctor? That way she'd have a husband *and* there would be a new doctor around here to take care of people when you get too old to do it."

So that was the plan.

The doctor decided to put together a test to determine both who would be the best one to be the next doctor *and* the best one to marry his daughter. He decided that he would pretend to be sick, and the one who could come up with the best cure for his imaginary ailments would be the winner.

One ailment alone wouldn't do it. No, the old doctor decided that he needed to be suffering from several things all at once. He thought about it for a few days and then announced his ailments.

"I'm feeling sick," he said one morning down at the community store. "I've lost my sense of taste, and that's not all. My memory's gone bad on me, too … I can't remember a thing! Besides that, I can't seem to tell the truth anymore. Every time I start to say something serious, a great big lie comes out of my mouth.

"Now," he went on, "if anybody can cure me of all three of these ailments at once, why, I reckon they deserve to marry my daughter. And, besides that, I also reckon they deserve to be the next doctor around these parts."

When people heard that, every man in the countryside started cooking up potions. It seemed that that doctor's girl was so good-looking that it inspired all kinds of original medical research. People from far and wide tried to cure the doctor's three made-up ailments, but no one tried anything which showed him that they were fit to marry his daughter or be the next doctor.

Finally, everybody in the country had tried and failed except Tom and Will and Jack.

They talked it over. Jack allowed as how he wasn't much for trying contests like this. He never had been, he said, because there was just too much tricking going on for anybody to get to win fair and square.

Tom and Will didn't think the same as Jack, though. They thought that one of them ought to be able to come up with an idea that would work. They talked about it late into the night, and finally each one of them got an idea about what he might try out on the doctor.

The next morning Tom got ready to try his plan. He told Jack and Will that he knew the old doctor was awful vain about women, and he thought he might be able to *insult* him into getting his memory back.

Tom walked down to the community store. The mail came in about the middle of the morning each day, and he knew that he would have a good audience when the old doctor came to pick his up. Finally the old man came, and while he was right in the middle of all his neighbors, Tom started talking.

"It's too bad about the old doctor, here," he said. "Why, he used to be a good doctor until he came down with these three ailments. Losing his taste and not being able to tell the truth … that's bad. But the worst thing is losing his memory. Yes, sir, it's hard to be a doctor when you can't remember what you're doing!"

Everybody was listening, including the doctor. Tom went on.

"Yes, the old doc here used to be awful good at doctoring *women*. Why, I've heard women say that he could cure them just by walking into the same room where they were." The doctor smiled when he heard this. He was awful proud that a lot of women of all ages were about half in love with him.

Tom kept talking. "Since his memory's gone, all that has changed. Why, I've heard that now the doctor can't tell one end of a woman from the other. I've heard that he can't remember which part does what. I've heard tell that he doesn't know one…"

"Wait a minute!" the old doctor cut Tom off right in the middle of his sentence. He had heard all he could stand.

"That's not true! I can remember as much about a woman as I ever have … in fact, more! You just ask old Missus …"

Then he caught himself and realized what he had just done as all of his friends broke out laughing to beat all!

"His memory's cured!" one of them said. *"And* he's telling the *truth!"* another added. "You've done a miracle, Tom! You ought to be put on right now as the new doctor!"

"Wait a minute," said the old doctor, who had recovered his humor by now. "What about my sense of taste? I still can't taste a thing in the world! You have to fix that before I'll call you a winner."

Tom went back home after that. At least, he thought, everybody had a good laugh. He told Will and Jack about his day, and they laughed all over again.

Will said, "His sense of taste is exactly what I'm going to work on. Wait until tomorrow and I'm going to take him on!"

The next morning Will got up early and started up to the doctor's house.

On the way he stopped off by where he knew a couple of men had a still for making corn whiskey. They had been moonshining all night and were just about to go home and sleep all day when Will showed up and begged then for a pint fruit jar of corn liquor.

"I need it to cure the doctor," he told them, and they all laughed even if they didn't have any idea about what kind of plan Will might have in mind.

Will slipped the pint of clear liquid inside the back of his hunting coat so it was out of sight when he walked up on the porch and knocked on the door of the doctor's house.

The doctor's wife came to the door. "I've come to cure the doctor of what ails him!" Will announced.

"Well," she frowned, "you've come awful early to cure him of anything ... he's still in the bed! I'll have to go get him up. He won't mind getting up if he's about to get cured."

"Then go get him," Will went on. "I've got some pills for him to take. Before you go, how about getting me a glass of water for him to take them with?"

The doctor's wife stepped into the kitchen and filled up a big water glass. She gave the water to Will and then disappeared into the back of the house to wake up the doctor.

As soon as she was out of sight, Will turned up the glass and drank every bit of the water in it. Then he pulled the pint jar of corn whiskey out of his coat and filled the water glass up with the clear liquor. That whiskey was so pure that if you didn't look close enough to notice it bead up on the top, you couldn't tell by sight that it wasn't water.

When the doctor and his wife came into the room, the doctor looked like he had been whipped out of bed against his will. He was rubbing his eyes and looked like he wasn't quite awake enough to stand upright, let alone walk.

"Hello, Will," the doctor said. "What ails you so early in the morning?"

"It's not me that's ailing, Doc," Will said. "It's you! And I've come here to cure you!" The doctor smiled when he remembered his made-up ailments.

"I've got some pills here that will cure anything," Will said. "They're kind of hard to swallow, though." He held the water glass of clear whiskey out to the doctor. "Here, Doc, take a good swig of this spring water and clear your throat before I give you the pills to take."

He handed the water glass full of corn liquor to the old doctor, and, half-asleep, the doctor gulped down a big swallow before he had a chance to realize what he was dealing with!

"WHOOooo!" the old doctor threw his head back and hollered. He danced all over the room and ran halfway up and down most of the walls before he could calm down enough to breathe in again.

"Lord, Will," the doctor said, "that wasn't *water* … that was about the stoutest corn liquor I've ever had!"

"See, Doc," Will laughed, *"you're cured* … and it didn't even take any pills! You're telling the truth, and you seem like you've got your sense of taste back as well."

"That's pretty good, Will," the doctor allowed. "Two out of three, just like your brother, what is his name? Oh, Will, my memory is still so bad ... what did I say that was that I just drank? Was it some tea from a church supper?"

"Your memory *is* bad, Doc," Will allowed. "I'm afraid I've done about the best I can. Somebody else will have to take it from here."

Will went home and told Jack and Tom about his day. They laughed their heads off just thinking about it.

By now everybody, even Tom and Will, had tried to cure the old doctor except for Jack. They kept poking at Jack, teasing him about getting to marry the doctor's daughter, asking him about whether he wanted to be a doctor or not, until finally Jack decided that maybe he just ought to go up to the doctor's house, have a go at curing the old man, and just get it over with.

The next morning Jack headed up toward the doctor's house to see what he could come up with. He didn't have a plan in mind at all. He just figured that some kind of idea would come to him along the way.

About halfway up to the doctor's house, Jack came to a field where a lot of sheep were being kept. There were a few lambs running around, and they all looked very nice to Jack. He liked to work with sheep.

Jack walked out into the field and scratched one of the lambs on the head. He figured that those sheep had been there for a while because there were sheep droppings all over the ground.

Jack thought out loud to himself, "Isn't it funny how an animal as big as a sheep has little old droppings like a rabbit! Why, these sheep droppings look like little old berries scattered all over the ground ... they're no bigger than pills the doctor would give you."

When he realized what he had said, Jack's own thoughts gave him an idea. He reached down and picked up about half a dozen of the roundest little sheep pellets he could find and slipped them into his coat pocket. Then he went on up to the doctor's house.

Jack knocked on the door, and when the doctor's wife opened it and he told her he had come to try to cure the doctor, she told him that the doctor was, of course, still in bed. She had Jack wait in the kitchen while she went in the back of the house to get her husband.

As soon as the doctor's wife disappeared out of the kitchen, Jack started looking around for the sugar bowl. He spotted it on a little cabinet, walked over, and lifted the cover off. Then Jack took those round sheep pellets out of his pocket, dropped them into the sugar bowl, and rolled them all around until they were completely covered with sugar. After that, they went straight back into Jack's pocket.

It took a few minutes for the doctor to pull some clothes on and come out of the bedroom. He was getting awful slow in the morning on these days. Finally he came out, spoke to Jack, and asked him what he had in mind.

"I came to cure you of what ails you, Doc. Whatever you've got, I've brought some pills that will take care of it. Now," said Jack, "tell me again just exactly what it is that is wrong with you?"

The old doctor had gotten smart through all the tricks people had pulled on him, and he thought Jack was trying to trick him into remembering that his memory was supposed to be one of his problems. So he said, "I can't remember all that's wrong with me, Jack, and if I could, I probably wouldn't tell you the truth about it. Jack, you'll just have to ask my wife here, or whoever this woman is, and she'll tell you what all my troubles are."

The doctor's wife was getting awful tired of this business, but she did go along with it. "He's just falling apart, Jack," she started. "He can't taste anything, his memory is completely gone, and, when he does have good sense, he can't tell the truth about *anything*. All three of those problems are getting him down all at once, Jack."

With that, Jack reached into his coat pocket and took out the sugar-coated sheep pellets. He handed two of them to the doctor.

"Here, Doc," he started in. "Take two of these, and be sure to chew them up before you swallow them."

The old doctor did exactly what Jack told him. He chewed, then swallowed hard with a terrible look on his face.

"Now, tell me, Doc," Jack asked him, "what did that medicine taste like?"

The doctor was just about choking from the awful taste, but he looked at Jack and answered, "Jack, if I didn't know better, I would say that I had just swallowed some sugar-coated sheep droppings!"

"Now, how about that?" Jack smiled. *"You are right!* Why, Doc, that means that your sense of taste is cured, *and* you are once again able to tell the truth. Isn't that just wonderful?"

The old doctor really choked now, but then he recovered himself and said to Jack, "What about my memory, Jack? Two out of three's not a full cure."

Jack held out his hand once more. "Just chew up two more of these pills, Doc!"

With that the old doctor stepped back and said, "That's all right, Jack ... one look at those pills and I think that my memory just got well, too!

"You win, Jack. You can marry my daughter, and, if you want to, you can be the next doctor."

And some people say that is just exactly what Jack did.

The Time Jack
Got the Silver Sword

One of the most common adventures I remember Jack having involved the various ways and times when he was employed as a giant killer. Sometimes, if the time for the story was short, Jack would dispatch one giant, get his due reward, and the story would be over. At other times, episodes could be strung together until Jack might kill half a dozen giants before the story came to an end. There was not one story of Jack killing giants; rather, this was a whole set of stories. The feeling was always that the giant was somehow not human, or so evil that the disposal was soundly applauded. Here is another story of a time Jack had to do away with some giants in order to get on toward his fortune.

One time Jack and Tom and Will and their mama and daddy were living in a little house that belonged to a big farmer. They had lived there a pretty long time, and Jack and his daddy and his brothers worked for the farmer on shares. They did manage to eat pretty well, but Jack thought that if they would load up and move on out toward the west, they might could get their own land and then make them a farm of their own.

Jack's daddy and his brothers weren't much in favor of this. They just wanted to stay right where they were and keep on at tenant farming. Jack's mama thought he was right, though, and as time went on she persuaded the others that this was actually the right thing for them all to do.

One day they told the farmer that they were going to leave, and in the next week they packed up everything that they had in a big old wagon that the farmer gave them. Then they got all their other things ready to head on out to look for a place of their own.

When the day came on which they had decided to leave, they hooked up their two old mules to the wagon, loaded up their last food and clothes, and headed out to the west.

Now, Jack and his family didn't exactly know where they were going. They had just heard that you could claim land if you went west and worked it, and that is what they planned to do. They traveled on for a few days and met several people who told them where there was some good land. The folks they met also told them that the good land was a little hard to get to.

The trouble, everybody told them, was that the good land lay on the other side of a big tract that belonged to the king. It wouldn't be so hard to get over there if you could cut across the king's land. But, since the king didn't like people cutting across his land, it was going to take about two weeks to go all the way around.

One day Jack and his family were talking about this with some people they met at a little store where they had stopped to buy some food. Finally, Jack's daddy asked a question to the store owner. "Couldn't we," he said, "couldn't we maybe just ask the king if we could just go across his land for a little shortcut? It's not like we were going to stay there or even hunt any of his animals. We wouldn't bother anything. Don't you think the king would let us do that?"

Then the whole truth came out.

"The real trouble is not the king," the store owner told them. "If you could get to where the king lives, I'm sure he would tell you just to go on through.

"The trouble is *giants*. There are three big, old, ugly, fourteen-foot-tall giants that have just taken over the king's land and are living up there. They kill and eat everything that moves, and that would include you if you cut across there and got caught.

"The only reason that they haven't killed and eaten the king and his family is that they live in a big house behind a high rock wall, and the giants are so big and heavy that they can't pull themselves up over the wall to get inside. Why, the king and his family are just like in prison up there. They can't come out from behind that wall or they would be eaten up in a minute!

"Now, you stay away from there ... go around!"

And so Jack and all his family kept going, way around the outside of the king's land. They surely didn't want to tangle with any fourteen-foot-tall, man-eating giants!

Everything went along quite well for about the next week. Then, though, they all started getting anxious to get on to set up their new home. And, after all, they hadn't seen or even heard any sign of those giants they were supposed to be afraid of.

Tom and Will came up with an idea. "Let's just take a little shortcut each day. Let's cut across a corner and go quiet and fast. We're never going to get on to our new land like this.

"We haven't even seen any giants. I think that man at the store just made that all up to scare us. Come on, let's cut across ... we'll never get there if we don't."

After a day or two of begging, the whole family decided to get along with it.

Early one morning they turned their mules and wagon off the path they had been following, and started to cut right across the king's land, heading straight for the west. They traveled all day. Then when it started to get dark, they weren't even halfway across to where they were supposed to come out.

Jack's daddy pulled the wagon with the mules into a little low laurel thicket at the base of a big rock cliff, and there they made plans for the night.

"We can't afford to take a chance on building a fire," he said. "Whoever might be out here would see us for sure. We better just eat some cold beans, and we'll get on out of here in the morning.

"And," he went on, "we'd better set up a lookout for the night."

Jack's daddy took the three boys up to the top of the hill above where he had hidden the mules and the wagon, and they picked out a big maple tree to hide up in to keep watch.

"I'll take the first turn," he said. "That'll be the most dangerous time. We'll switch off about every three hours. Tom and then Will. Jack will be the last in the morning. There's not likely to be much trouble when the light's coming back in the morning.

"Whoever is up here better keep the gun with him. Now you boys go back and sleep where your mama is until time for Tom's turn."

The three boys went back down to the wagon while Jack's daddy set up for the first watch.

Nothing at all happened through that first watch, and so Jack's daddy came on down to sleep at the wagon while Tom went up to keep his watch. Tom sat up in that tree and didn't see anything either. He came down to sleep after his time was up, and then Will went on up there. Of course, Will didn't see or hear a thing; and when it was time for Jack to take the last watch, there was only about an hour to go before it would start to get daylight.

They all thought things were probably safe by now, but they still sent Jack on up there so he could have a turn at keeping watch just like the others had.

Jack climbed way up in the same big maple tree where his brothers had been for their turns. He sat there, holding his daddy's gun across his lap, and didn't hear a sound but the wind in the trees while the dark gradually faded and the light of day slipped into the woods. He thought that he'd wait just a few more minutes and then he'd go on back down to the camp where the others were.

About then, though, Jack thought he heard something coming from way down below in the woods. He got real still and strained his ears to listen. Sure enough, he could hear somebody talking and feet shuffling along through the leaves and brush on the ground.

As the voices got louder, Jack looked toward the direction of the sound. Then he saw who it was. Coming up through the woods right toward the tree where he was hiding walked *three* giants that must each one be at least fourteen feet tall.

As soon as Jack could see them, he could also tell what they were carrying. One of them had two cows slung over his shoulders. It looked like he had wrung their necks like chickens and had just slung them over his shoulders to carry them.

The second one had what looked to Jack like a handful of garden tools. He had spades and turning forks and big saws. Then Jack realized that what he was seeing was not a bundle of tools, but a set of knives and forks and spoons just big enough for these giants to eat with.

The last giant was carrying a big, black iron cooking pot. He had it upside down over his head so it was resting on his shoulders by the rim and was covering his head completely up. He couldn't see a thing about where he was going, and he kept running into trees over and over again. He kept telling the first two that it was time for them to take a turn at carrying the pot ... it was giving him a headache!

"Well, there," Jack thought, "they may be big, but from what I have seen so far, they are also mighty *dumb!* Maybe I don't have to be so scared of them after all."

The giants came right on up to under the very tree where Jack was perched. Then they threw their loads down on the ground and sat down and started talking with one another.

"I shore am hongry!" the first one said.

Then the second one said, "I shore am hongry!"

After that the third one said, "I don't know about you'all, but I shore am hongry!"

Jack thought, "They *are* dumb! If I'm careful, I don't think they really are much to worry about."

About then it was all the way daylight, and Jack could really get a good look at what these big boys looked like.

The youngest one had a head full of black hair and a long, black beard that flopped against his chest when he talked. The middle one was as red-headed as he could be. He was either clean-shaven or else his beard just never had come in to begin with. The oldest one was as bald as a turnip, but he did have a droopy, gray-looking moustache which hung down around his mouth.

They were such a funny-looking bunch that Jack had a hard time not laughing right out loud just looking at them.

While he was watching them from his perch up in the tree, the giants had started to cook the cows for their breakfast.

They carried water from a little creek, filled up the pot, and then built a fire and started boiling the two cows whole—hair, hide, teeth, horns, hooves, eyeballs, and all. Jack couldn't believe that they were going to eat such as that!

They boiled those two old cows until the meat started to fall apart.

By now Jack had seen about all he wanted to see. Besides, he figured if he could slip out of here and get on down to where his family was, they could slip on out of there while the giants were eating. It was so daylight that he was starting to worry that his daddy would come up here looking for him and might walk right into the middle of these giants.

The only trouble was that every time he started to ease down out of the tree, the limbs started cracking and leaves would fall. He figured he needed to get the giants distracted, and then he could slip on down.

Jack had brought his slingshot in his pocket along with a handful of sharp-edged flint rocks he had picked up the day before. He always kept his slingshot with him in case he needed a weapon. He loaded up a rock and got ready.

The biggest one of the giants took one of those giant forks and jabbed a big piece of meat with it. While he was holding the meat over the pot and blowing on it to cool it off, Jack pulled back and shot at the chunk of meat. It fell back into the pot and splashed boiling juice all over that big old giant. He was storming mad and thought for sure that one of his brothers had caused it.

"I don't know who did that, or how," the giant said to his brothers, "but you better not do it again or you'll be sorry for sure!" The other two said that they didn't do it, but he didn't believe them at all. He jabbed up another hunk of that cow and started to put it in his mouth.

Jack pulled back with another rock and shot the old giant smack in the back of the hand. The giant jerked so hard that he stabbed that fork right into his own cheek.

"Now, quit it!" he hollered at his brothers.

"We didn't do nothing!" both of them fussed right back at him.

"Well, I reckon you did!" the big one went on. "Somehow you'all like to have caused me to put my eye out! Now, don't mess with me again or I'll crack both of your heads!"

The two brothers just sat there and looked dumb.

The big old giant put down the fork and picked up the big, shovel-sized spoon. He ladled up a big spoonful of the hot juice. Jack didn't even want to think about what he thought he saw floating in it. The giant blew on the spoon of cow soup once or twice.

As he lifted it toward his mouth, Jack was loaded again. He let loose with a flint rock and knocked that spoonful of hot broth right in the old giant's face.

This time the giant didn't even fuss. He just slung the spoon out into the woods and jumped right on his brothers. They were fighting and scratching and biting to beat the band, and while they were scrapping it out, old Jack was slipping down out of that tree so he could get on out of there in a hurry.

In the midst of all of that ruckus, those giants couldn't see or hear a thing besides their own fighting, and Jack made it all the way down to the bottom of the tree. He was ready to step down to the ground and beat it out of there when the last limb he stepped on broke with a loud *crack*. Those giants stopped their fighting and looked straight at Jack. He couldn't do a thing but look back at them. He was purely scared to death.

"Look, there's a little boy!" the first giant said.

Then the middle giant said, "Look, there's a little boy!"

"Hey, look, you'all," the third giant said, "there's a little boy!"

When Jack heard all three giants say the same thing over and over, he remembered how dumb they were, and he wasn't so scared anymore.

He looked right at the giants and said, "You can call me a little boy if you want to, *little men,* but there are a lot of things I can do that you can't do!"

"What can you do that I can't do?" the oldest giant asked Jack.

"If you're so smart, *you* figure it out!" he answered.

The giants were so dumb that instead of jumping on Jack, they did, in fact, sit there and try to figure out something that Jack might do that they couldn't do.

They mumbled to one another for a few minutes, then went over to Jack and picked him up.

"We've got it figured out, Jack! We know exactly what you can do that we can't do. Come on with us ... you're going to get us into the king's castle lands!"

Jack didn't know what they were talking about. He also didn't want to go with them. But he didn't have any choice about that since they had already picked him up, and the biggest one had him under his ugly arm.

Jack knew that his daddy and Tom and Will would come up to the lookout tree any time now to see why he hadn't come back to the camp. He also knew that they would not find a thing to tell them that he was alive and, so far, well. He couldn't imagine what they would think when they found nothing but a big cooking pot full of cow bones left under the maple tree.

The giants seemed to be getting pretty excited about wherever they were taking Jack because they went faster and faster as they carried him through the woods. They passed him back and forth whenever the one who was carrying him got tired, and a time or two they almost made a little game out of throwing Jack around.

"Watch out!" Jack hollered when they almost dropped him on one toss. "If you kill me, you won't know whether I can do *it* or not." (He didn't have any idea what "it" was, but his warning to the giants seemed to work.)

Finally, they came up over a big hill, and up ahead Jack began to see something strange showing up through the trees.

At first he thought it was a low rock cliff, but then as they got closer he could see that it was actually a man-made rock wall. The wall was about twenty to thirty feet high and was so long that it just faded out of sight in the woods long before Jack could see either the end of it or where it made a turn.

"Here we are," the biggest giant said.

"Well, here we are," said the middle giant.

Jack knew what was coming next. The youngest giant said, "Hey, boys, here we are."

They carried Jack on along the wall until they came close to a place where a huge wooden gate was closed fast. Then they walked back down from the gate a little way until they came to the spot where the wall seemed to be the shortest.

"Here we are, little boy," the oldest of the giants said to Jack. Of course the other two went on and also said the same thing, but Jack was getting a little tired of hearing everything three times by now, so he didn't pay any attention to it.

"We've been wanting to get into the king's castle lands for a long time now, but we're so big and strong we can't get up over this wall." The biggest of the giants was doing all the talking now. "We are awful glad that you told us you could do stuff we can't do or we never would have figgered this out.

"Now, little boy, what we are going to do is to *throw* you over this wall. When you come down on the other side, you run up to that big old gate up there and open it up and let us get in."

The oldest of the giants now handed Jack over to his younger brothers to do the throwing. They got hold of Jack by his arms and legs and swung him back and forth a few times to warm up. Then they let go, and Jack went sailing up through the air like a little rock, just flying over that wall like there was nothing to him at all.

What neither Jack nor the giants could see from the ground was how wide the wall was. When Jack got up to flying through the air, he saw that the wall was a good twenty feet thick. It was so wide that the top was almost like a road, except that there was grass growing up all over it.

That thick wall just may have saved Jack's life because, instead of flying all the way over it and then having to fall all the way down to the ground, Jack happened to land right on top of the wall in the middle of some high grass. He looked down at the giants and waved to them to show them how well he had landed.

All three of the big old giants cheered for Jack, and even he was right proud of himself.

"Now, little boy, get down on the other side and go on up to the gate. We will wait for you right up there on the outside."

Every so far along the inside of the big wall there was either a ramp or a set of stair steps going down to the inside ground, so it was no problem at all for Jack to go on down to the ground. He didn't know exactly what he was going to do next, so he walked up toward the gate where the giants were just to get a look at what held it shut.

When he got there, he saw a sort of big tunnel through the wall, with the gate right outside of it. The gate was held shut by a big beam which was slipped down into some brackets on the doors. All you needed to do to open it was just to lift up that beam, and the doors would be free to open.

The giants on the outside already were hollering through the gate to Jack before he even got there. "Come on, little boy, open the gate. Let us get on in there right now!"

Jack knew that no matter what he decided to do, opening the gate was not going to be part of his plan.

He got up to the gate and started banging around on it and rattling some of the hardware that was there on the inside. He also started huffing and snorting like he was trying mighty hard to lift or move something heavy. The giants got real quiet as they listened and tried to imagine what Jack must be doing.

Finally Jack hollered out to the giants, "Well, boys, I'm not having any luck in letting you'all in. I see exactly how to open the gate, but the latch is rusted shut because it's been closed up for so long and I can't bust it loose.

"You'all wait right here, and I will go scout around some and see if I can find something that I can knock it loose with. The old giants all agreed and sat down to wait on the outside.

Jack was not sure where he was or what he was going to do, but at least he was safe from the giants for a little while. He started following the road that led in from the gate to see where he was and who or what he could find.

In no time at all, Jack rounded a curve in the road, and there in front of him was the biggest house he had ever seen. It just had to be the king's castle house.

Jack walked up to the castle house and was just amazed by the size of it. It needed a lot of work, though, and Jack reckoned that being shut up in here because of those giants—even having a lot of gold—wouldn't do a king much good. He walked up on the front porch.

It was still fairly early in the morning, and it seemed like everybody was still asleep, as Jack didn't hear a sound coming from anywhere. He thought he would just walk around a little bit and check things out.

When he came to the front door, it was standing wide open, and Jack began to wonder if anybody actually lived there or not. He didn't stop to think that with a big wall around everything, there wasn't any point in even closing the door at night.

Jack walked on in and found himself inside a big hall that was bigger than any house he had ever been in before. There was all kinds of furniture and old stuff just everywhere.

While Jack was looking around, he saw something on the wall that he got real interested in. It was a great big, long silver sword that looked just as sharp as it could be.

Jack thought, "If I had that sword, I could go back down there and maybe take those giants on a little bit."

He tried to pick the sword up from where it was hanging on the wall, but it was so heavy that he couldn't budge it. Then he saw the sign that was hanging on the wall beside the sword.

It said, "Whoever is strong enough to drink the draught is strong enough to heft the sword." Jack looked all around there but didn't see anything to drink, so he figured that it was just some old saying of some kind from a long time ago.

"Too bad," Jack thought, and then he started exploring around the castle house some more.

Every door was standing wide open, and so Jack could either see or just wander around through all the rooms as much as he wanted to.

He went on to one big room where he heard some snoring, and there, right in the bed with his crown hanging on the bedpost, was the old king himself. In the next room the queen was asleep. Jack thought it sure was a waste of rooms to have the king and queen taking up two whole rooms for nothing but sleeping.

He wandered down the hall and into another room. All of a sudden he looked over at the bed and saw a girl sleeping in there. Jack didn't know that he had stumbled onto the only daughter of the old king himself.

She was so pretty that when Jack saw her he had to grab onto the wall to keep from passing right out on the floor. Every time he looked at her he about lost his breath, but he just couldn't keep from looking again. Why, he never did know that girls could be made this pretty, and she was not even awake.

Then Jack saw a glass bottle on a shelf on the wall. The bottle was dark colored and had a cork in the top, and over it there was a sign on the wall. The sign said, "Whoever is strong enough to give in to love, is strong enough to drink the draught."

Jack wasn't sure just what this meant, but after what looking at this girl had done to him, he needed something to drink.

He picked up the glass bottle and pulled the cork out of it. When he did, smoke came out with a sound like it was fuming around on the inside. Still, Jack turned it up to take a drink.

When he did, what came out of the bottle was the most wonderful-tasting liquid he'd ever had. It was sweet and pure and smooth and clear, and it tickled as it ran across his tongue. Jack drank the whole bottle without stopping and wondered why nobody else had drunk from the bottle, as good as it tasted to him.

This time when he looked back at the sleeping king's daughter, he didn't get dizzy. He just knew now, though, that it was time to go get rid of those giants so these people could get back to living the way they were supposed to.

Jack went marching back out through the big hall of the house, and, as he passed that silver sword, he reached out and just grabbed the handle.

When he did, the sword came right off the wall into his hand, and this time it felt as light as a feather. Why, it was about seven feet long, and still Jack could swing it around his head until it made the air whistle. He started out the door with the sword and headed down the road to where the giants were.

Jack did a little thinking on his way back to the big gate. He figured that with this sword he could take on any one of the three giants, but he began to realize that trying to take on all three at one time might be a little too much for him. So he started trying to come up with a plan.

Jack had noticed a little low tunnel down close to where he had first come off of the wall, and when he checked it out he saw what it was.

About fifty yards down the wall from the big gate there was a little late-night tunnel for people in the old days who got shut out of the castle walls after the gates were closed for the night. It was a low tunnel, not big enough for somebody to ride a horse through, and narrow enough that it would just take one soldier to guard it. Jack thought that it was probably just big enough for the giants to be able to crawl through, one at a time, on their knees. Now he knew what to do.

He walked back up to where they were waiting for him on the other side of the big gate. Jack didn't say anything about having the big silver sword. He just told the giants that he was back to try to get them inside the castle land.

While the giants listened, Jack told them that he just couldn't find anything that could help him get the gate opened, but that he had found another way they could get through the wall. He told them that there was a little crawly-tunnel right down the wall from where they were, and that if they would come on down there he would show them exactly how to get in.

The giants were really anxious to get inside by now, and they followed the sound of Jack's voice as he led them down the wall to the late-night tunnel.

Old Jack actually crawled most of the way through the low tunnel until the three giants could see him from the outside. Then he told them that if they would crawl through the low tunnel one at a time, he would have a real surprise waiting for them on the inside.

Those giants all wanted in there so badly that they had to fight for a little while before they could decide which one got to crawl through the passageway first. Finally, the big old one with the black hair won out, and he started in through the hole.

Jack could both see him coming and tell which one it was because he could just see the top of his dirty black hair as he scrunched on his belly to get in through the late-night crawly-hole.

Jack picked up the seven-foot-long silver sword, and, when that black-headed giant's head came popping out of that hole, you can just guess what happened to it!

The other two giants wanted to know why the first one was not crawling on through the hole. Jack hollered out to them that he was stuck and they would have to push him on through. They did, and then Jack could see the bald-headed one coming next.

In no time there was not a giant in the king's whole land who had not lost his head to that old silver sword.

About that time Jack heard horses coming, and, when he looked up, here came the king and all his men riding down there on their horses. They had seen that the silver sword was gone when they got up in the morning and were out looking for the man powerful enough to handle it.

When they saw that it was little old Jack, then they knew that it was the power of the love draught and not his own natural strength that had done away with the giants. So they loaded Jack up and took him right back up there to the castle house where that beautiful king's daughter was just having her breakfast.

When she saw Jack, she told her daddy that he was just the boy she had been dreaming about the night before; and by noon, it was agreed that Jack was going to stay on there and marry her.

Jack was so excited about all of this that he almost forgot to go back and hunt up his mama and daddy and Tom and Will. But he did remember after a while, and he went back through the woods with some of the king's men and found them.

They were awful upset about Jack being gone, but when they saw him and then heard about the whole story, they were glad to stop and settle right there on the king's land, and some people say that they are living right on there to this very day.

The Time Jack Learned About Old and New

*One of the main reasons for my wanting to put together this collection about Jack is my feeling that most folklorists collecting Jack tales miss the full stories as they are told in a community in which **time** is of no concern to the teller or the hearer. What I experience in reading many collections compiled by outside visitors are quick summaries telling **about** stories rather than the full tellings of these stories that happen when no one cares whether they are even finished tonight ... because they will be told again. The following is a fully told-out story about Jack. It could be ended at several points, if time required, but I present it here as I remember it told when nobody was in a hurry. It also shows how some themes wander from story to story and are not strictly confined to a particular adventure.*

A long time ago old Jack was just living along at home with his mama and his two older brothers Tom and Will. Their daddy was at this time either gone off or dead—nobody for sure knows which—and so Jack's mama had to take care of all three of those boys all by herself. It was a job, to be sure!

Time went on, and finally the years passed until Tom and Will were all grown up. Still, they were just lying around the house and doing nothing at all to help their mama or take care of themselves.

Finally their mama got tired of this, and one day she came to Will and said, "Will, you are all grown up and able to do about anything you would put your mind to. It is time for you to get on out of here and make your own fortune and just start living on your own.

"You just get yourself ready to go on out of here tomorrow and make your own way in the world."

With that, she began to hunt up some things and put together a little pack of stuff to help him out along the way.

While she was packing up Will's things, their mama was fixing supper, and she put a big Dutch oven full of cornbread batter in the coals of the fire so it could bake. About that time she realized that she didn't have an extra needle and thread that she could send with Will so he could sew on buttons and patch his clothes.

So she said to Will, "Will, I am going up to the neighbor's house to see if they have a needle and thread that I can send with you to patch your clothes. I'm going to take Tom and Jack with me, but you stay here and keep getting your things packed up.

"I want you to watch this pan of cornbread, and don't let it burn while we are gone. While you're at it, you might as well clean up around the house and get things fixed up so that we'll be ready to eat when we get back." Then she and Tom and Jack went on out the door and on their way.

Just about as soon as they got out of sight, a little drawn-up, humped-over old woman came hopping out of the woods and right up to the door of their house. She must have been some kind of magic woman, because right outside the door she reached down and scooped up a handful of dust from the ground. Then she threw the dust up in the air into the wind, and the wind blew it all over her. As that dust covered her, she started changing in her appearance.

First she began to straighten up and get taller and bigger; then she changed into looking like a man. Her beard grew out and her ragged clothes turned into rich-looking robes until, finally, she looked just exactly like the old king of that land himself! Then she, looking just like the king, walked right up to the door of Jack's house and knocked on it.

Will opened the door. He sure was surprised to see the king right there at his house.

"Why, King!" he said, "come right in. I sure am glad that you stopped in. What can I do for you today?"

The king talked right back to Will. "I was just out walking over my land, Will, and I got sort of tired and hungry. I was wondering if maybe I could just stay here a while and maybe get a little something to eat for my supper."

"Why, sure," Will answered him. "You just sit right down here in this rocking chair and rock. I'm just watching after supper and cleaning up the house a little for my mama. As soon as she and my brothers get home, we can all eat supper."

The king asked Will, "Can I do anything to help you out while we wait?"

"*Oh, no!*" Will said. "You're the *king*! You just sit there and rock in that chair and I'll take care of everything. Come to think of it, I'll just go out and milk the cow before Mama gets back so she won't have to milk in the dark. I *do* like to help my mama."

Will never had milked a cow before, but he was determined to make a good impression on the king. He was out there so long trying to get some milk, before he realized that he just couldn't do it and gave up, that the cornbread was burned up hard as a rock when he came back in the house.

Will came back in the house, and there was smoke everywhere. The king was just sitting there being the king, like

Will had told him to. Will tried to pull the bread out of the fire and save some of it, but it was too late!

The old king said, "Will, I believe that I'll just go on down the road and eat somewhere else, if it's all the same to you." Then the one who sure had looked just like the king slipped out the door and was gone.

In a little while Jack and Tom and Mama came back from the neighbor's house with a needle and some thread. They all sat down to eat supper. Will brought out the burned bread.

They tried to poke some of the middle out of the blackened bread and eat it, but all of the crust and most of the middle was too hard to eat.

Will never did say a single word about the king's being there … or about his trying to milk.

The next morning everybody told Will goodbye, and he started out on his own to seek his fortune. Will got along all right on his own, as far as anybody knows, but he didn't do anything great. In fact, that's the last time most people saw or heard from him for as long as they could remember.

It wasn't very long, as time passed, until Jack's mama started pestering Tom to get on out on his own and make his fortune, too. He never did do anything about it until finally one day she just told him it was time to get on the road.

"Tomorrow's going to be your day to go, Tom. You've been lying around here long enough. It's time for you to get on out of here and start taking care of yourself. I'll pack a few things up for you to take with you and help you out on the way."

She began to pack up a few things for Tom while she was fixing supper. While all of this was going on, she, as usual, mixed up the big Dutch oven full of cornbread and put it in the fire-coals.

About the time she got the bread on the fire, she realized she didn't have a jug for Tom to carry water in, so she said, "Tom, I'm going to take Jack with me and go up to the neighbor's house to see if I can borrow a jug for you to carry water in.

"You watch that bread, and don't let it burn like Will did. While you're waiting here, you might as well straighten up the house and fix things up so we can eat soon as we get back ... but don't let that bread burn!"

Then she and Jack lit out down the road to the neighbor's house.

Now, just as soon as they got out of sight, that same dried-up, doubled-over old woman who had visited Will came creaking out of the woods. She pulled that same trick all over again and turned herself into the king. Then she invited herself to eat with Tom.

"Can I help you out while we're waiting for supper to get done?" the king asked Tom. Tom was looking awful busy, watching that bread and rearranging all the mess in the house so the king would think he was working.

"On, no!" Tom said. "You're the king! You're not supposed to work. You just sit there in that rocking chair and rock a little, if you want to. I can handle all of this.

"Why, while I'm all stirred up to work, I think I'll run out and milk the cow and feed the chickens so I'll still have time to change the beds before Mama gets home. I sure do like to help my mama."

So the king just sat there and rocked. Tom did feed the chickens, but while he was trying to milk the cow, the cornbread burned up as hard as a rock.

The old king was standing in the door when Tom came back from the barn. He said, "I think I'll just go on and eat somewhere else, Tom. All that fresh milk you've got won't be very good with burned cornbread." So the one who looked like the king again went on his way.

Just about then Jack and his mama got home. They just threw that burned bread out and ate some old cold left-over bread. Jack's mama seemed like she was in a big hurry to get Tom packed up with his water-jug so he could get on his way the next day.

Like Will, Tom didn't say a single word to show that the king had ever been there.

The next morning he went on his way. Tom did pretty well seeking his fortune, as far as we know. At least he didn't come begging back home. Actually, nobody much ever heard from him from then on.

After this, Jack and his mama just lived on there for a good little while. Jack was awful good to help his mama, not like Tom and Will. He knew how to milk the cow; he knew just how much to feed the chickens; and he was a pretty good cook as well. They got along just fine.

Then one day Jack came to his mama and said, "Mama, I think it's about time that I lit out on my own and started seeking my fortune. I need to get on my own and start looking out for myself."

"Oh, no, Jackie," his mama said. "You can just stay right on here with me. I've got plenty of room for both of us."

"No, Mama," Jack went on, "I have to learn to take care of myself. You won't always be here, and I have to seek my own fortune.

"I believe that I'll pack up my stuff, and tomorrow I'll just hit the road for a while."

With that, Jack started getting together a few things that he wanted to take with him. While he was doing this, his mama was fixing supper. She had just mixed up the cornbread and put it in the Dutch oven in the fire when Jack came up to her and said, "Mama, I've got my stuff all ready to go, but I don't have a sack to carry it in."

"Well, sir," his mama said, "you just watch this bread so it won't burn up, and I'll run to the neighbor's house and see if I can borrow a sack for you. Don't worry about doing anything else around the house while I'm gone … just watch the bread, will you? We'll eat as soon as I get back." Then she took out for the neighbor's house.

Sure enough, just as soon as Jack's mama was out of sight, right out of the woods came hobbling that scrunched-up little old magic woman. Right off, she turned herself into looking just like the old king. Then she knocked on the door of Jack's house.

Jack opened the door. Of course he didn't know anything at all about the visits that had been made to Tom and Will before they had left home. As far as he knew, he was the first one of all to get to see the king.

"Come in, King!" Jack said. He was excited. "I am so glad that you have stopped by! I guess you're out walking over your land, are you? How about staying a little bit and then eating supper with us?"

"That's just what I was hoping for," said the king. "I think I'll just sit down here in this rocking chair while the supper finishes cooking. I don't guess there's anything I can help you do in the meantime, is there, Jack?"

"Well," Jack said, "now that you mention it ... I sure would like to feed and milk before my mama gets back to the house, but I do need to be sure that the bread doesn't burn up. How about if you watch the bread for me while I feed and milk?"

"Well, sure, Jack," the king said.

"And," Jack went on, "while you not doing anything else, how about setting the table and maybe straightening the house up a little while I'm out at the barn? And if you finish with that, I know my mama sure could use some wood chopped before I have to go on my way tomorrow!"

Between the work that Jack did and the work that the king was recruited to do, the whole house was in fine shape in no time.

Jack's mama came home in a little while. The cornbread was just right. The king had taken it out of the fire just at the right time. Jack and his mama and the king all had a big supper and a fine evening.

After supper the three of them were all sitting around and talking when the king spoke up. "Jack," he said, "you know that I'm really not the king at all." Then he picked up a feather duster and began to dust himself off. As the dust flew off, his robes turned into rags, his beard disappeared, and he changed from looking like the king back into that little old dried-up-looking woman. She looked like she could have been a hundred years old.

"Bedads!" Jack fairly hollered, "you must be some kind of magic! I wish Tom and Will could have seen this."

"They could have, Jack," said the old woman. "Yes, they surely could have. But they were both working so hard to impress the king that they didn't have time to take notice of anything … and then, that king didn't stay until you got home.

"But you, Jack, you're different. *You're the only one around here who knows that when something needs to be done, it doesn't matter who does it!*"

"Well," Jack smiled, "I never thought about that."

"Of course you didn't, Jack," said the old woman, smiling now. "Because you are so clever, I am going to see that you finally do get to meet the real king. And I am going to give you something to take with you when you go to seek your fortune that will help you out all along the way."

From way down in an old leather bag, she pulled out a little, round, flattened glass bottle about the size of a big pocket watch. The bottle had a little cap on the side where the winding-stem on a watch would be. She handed the bottle to Jack.

"What's this?" Jack asked her.

"It's a *Death's-eye glass.*"

"What's that?"

"If somebody is sick, you can fill it up with some of the same water they have been drinking, cap it up and shake it, warm it in your hands, then hold it up to your eye and look through it at the person who is sick in the bed.

"If you see a skeleton standing at the foot of the bed, then Death has come close, but the person will get well. But, Jack, if the skeleton is standing right up there at the head of the bed, then Death has come to stay and that person will surely die."

Jack thought to himself, "I don't know what good that thing will be to me. She should have given me some gold." But he thanked her and put the bottle in his pocket.

Finally the old woman left. Jack finished packing up all of his stuff in a big flour sack his mama had got from the neighbors. Then, after a good night's sleep, he told his mama goodbye and started out making his own way into the world.

Jack had a lot of big adventures on his way through the world, and he made a few little fortunes as he went along on his own. Everything seemed to be working out right well for him. Sometimes it was right boring, his life was running along so well.

Then one day he came into a little town in a land that was pretty far off from where he had left home. He went right up into an inn and bought himself something to eat and drink. He wasn't as much hungry as he was wanting to just listen in to what the people who lived around there were talking about. That way he could find out if there was anything nearby that he could get into.

Everybody he listened to was talking about the same thing. Every conversation he heard was about the king's daughter.

It seemed to Jack like the king's daughter was bad sick and that nothing anybody tried to do seemed to help her get well. The old king of this land had sworn to everybody that he would give half of his kingdom to anybody who could cure her, and more. Why, whoever could cure the king's daughter would get to *marry* her and then be the next king.

"Well," Jack thought, "that sounds like just the right thing for me."

Then he heard the hard news. Anyone who tried to cure the king's daughter and failed would have his head cut right off. It seemed that the king didn't want anybody messing around with his daughter who didn't know what he was doing.

"Shoot," Jack thought when he heard that, "I might as well try anyway. Risking having your head cut off is a lot better than being just bored to death."

So Jack finished his dinner and then lit right out of there for the king's house.

Jack didn't really have any idea what he was going to do. That didn't matter to him. He knew that some kind of idea would come to him.

He knocked right on the king's door, and the king himself answered it. Before the king even had a chance to say hello to Jack, Jack himself spoke up. "I've come to cure your daughter, King."

"Who are you?" said the king.

"I'm Jack!"

"Well, Jack," the king answered him, "I reckon your head won't be on much longer."

"Just take me to your daughter," Jack puffed up.

The old king took Jack up into a pretty bedroom where his daughter was stretched out in the bed. She looked like she was awful close to death. But even half-dead, this king's girl was more beautiful than any other well girl Jack had ever seen. He just wished he could figure out something to do before his head got cut off.

He stuck his hands in his pockets to think, and, just as he noticed the water pitcher beside her bed, Jack felt the little round Death's-eye glass in his pocket.

Then Jack's thoughts began to rub together. "Is that your daughter's drinking water?" he asked the king.

"Yes it is … when she can drink any," the king answered.

Jack pulled the little bottle out and uncapped it on the side. Then he dribbled the bottle full of water, capped it up, and shook it. He warmed it in his hands as he stood back to where he could see the whole room.

Jack held the Death's-eye glass up to one eye, closed the other eye, and looked through the glass. "Oh, Oh …" he thought, "What will I ever do now?" There was a big old skeleton standing right there at the head of the bed just fixing to pick the life right out of the king's daughter's body and run off with it.

Since nobody else could see the skeleton, nobody could figure out what Jack was doing when he picked up a big fire-poker by the fireplace and went toward the head of the bed. He was swinging that poker with one hand and holding the bottle up to his eye with the other hand.

Jack whacked that skeleton's skull right off, and it hit the wall and fell into a little pile of dust. Then he knocked that skeleton all to pieces and it fell all over the floor in little piles of dust. People were coughing and choking all over that room!

When the dust died down and all the coughing stopped, there was the king's daughter, sitting right up on the side of the bed, as well and as healthy as she had ever been in her whole life.

The old king cried some, and he kissed her some; then he said to Jack, "Come on down to my counting house, Jack. It's time to get your reward."

Jack followed him down there, and the king had two wagons loaded up with bags of gold. He said to Jack, "That's half the treasure in all of my kingdom. I do thank you for curing my daughter ... even if I don't exactly know how you did it."

"Wait a minute!" Jack said. "What about getting to marry your daughter and be the next king?"

The old king choked a little; then he said, "Now, Jack, you know I can't do that! Why, you're just a little old boy right off of the road. I don't even know where you were born or who your mama and daddy are. I just can't let you marry my daughter."

"You promised," said Jack, "and everybody knows it."

"I guess you are right about that, Jack. But before you can marry her, you are going to have to prove that you are smart enough to take care of her.

"I will have to give you three tests, and if you can pass those, then I'll know that you are fit to marry her."

"Well, let's get started," said Jack.

"You just wait until tomorrow," said the king. "Then I will start you off on the first test."

They all had a big supper at the king's house. Then Jack went upstairs and went to sleep.

Along sometime in the night, Jack felt somebody pulling on his sleeve. He opened his eyes, and there, beside his bed, stood the king's daughter. She was more beautiful than Jack had even remembered.

"Jack," she whispered, "Jack … if you want to marry me, then be careful what you do tomorrow. I don't know what my daddy has in mind, but if he offers you something old and something new, you be sure to take whatever looks *old*."

"Well, sure," said Jack. Then he fell right back to sleep.

After breakfast the next morning the old king took Jack out in the back of the house where it looked like a whole forest of big hickory trees had been cut down and sawed up into two-foot lengths. The wood was just lying around all over the place.

"Now, Jack," said the king, "a couple of days ago, some of my men and I cut down these twelve big hickory trees and sawed them up so they could be split into firewood for the winter. I dropped my pocket watch somewhere in there while we were sawing, and I'm scared to death that if I don't find it before it rains, it'll ruin.

"How about just splitting up all this wood and stacking it up to one side and then finding my watch for me?"

"Why, sure!" said Jack. "Is this my first test?"

"It is, Jack. Now here are two go-devils and some wedges for you to split with."

The king held out two go-devils for Jack to pick from. The go-devils were like sledge hammers except that one side was sharp instead of flat.

One of the go-devils was brand new, about a ten-pounder, with a long, smooth, straight ash handle. The other one had been used so much that the head was all squashed out, and the sharp side was all chipped up. Besides all that, the old handle on it was split, and Jack just knew that one lick with the old split-handled tool would blister his hands all over.

So Jack reached right out and took that big, new go-devil, picked up a splitting wedge, and started to work.

He split that first cut just fine, but when he was working on the second one, he noticed that all the pieces of the first one had jumped back together. Not only that, they had jumped back to make not just one un-split cut of log, but two!

The harder and faster Jack worked, the faster that pile of unsplit wood got bigger and bigger. By the middle of the day, the whole pile of wood was at least twice as big as it had been to start with.

About noontime the king's daughter showed up. She was bringing Jack some food for his lunch. "What in the world are you doing, Jack? Where did all this pile of wood come from?"

"You just don't know," Jack said, almost fussing. "I'm working so hard that by this evening there'll be enough wood here to make firewood for two or three winters, if anybody around here can split it up!"

"Jack," the king's daughter kept on, "which go-devil are you using?"

"I'm using the only one that looked like it's worth anything!"

Then the king's daughter reached behind her and pulled out the old split-handled go-devil. Jack shook his head, but he took it and gave it a try.

As soon as Jack took one swing with the go-devil, it jumped right out of his hands and took over on its own. It split wood left and right. Every time it split one cut, another one just fell apart. And, as that wood was split, it just flew into neat stacks right along the side of the back yard.

In about thirty minutes from the start, it was done, all but one last cut of wood. Jack walked over to it, and there, right on top of it, was the king's lost pocket watch!

Jack called the old king out of the house, showed him the pile of wood, and gave him his watch.

"Well, I'll be switched, Jack. You sure are something. Tomorrow I'm really going to try you out!"

That night Jack had a big supper, then went on upstairs to sleep. He was just about worn out from this first big test.

Way in the night Jack felt somebody tugging on his hair and calling to him, "Jack ... Jack ..." He opened his eyes, and there beside his bed stood the king's daughter.

"Jack," she said, "if you have any idea that you want to get married to me, then, tomorrow, whatever my daddy does, if he offers you something old and something new, you take what looks *old*. Do you think you can remember that?"

"Yes," Jack said. Then he fell back to sleep.

The next morning the old king got hold of Jack right after breakfast and took him for a walk along the road that ran from town up to his big house. "Just look at all those ditch-banks, Jack.

"Those ditch-banks are so all grown up there with weeds and sprouts and nettles that there could be snakes and hornets' nests and all kinds of wild things in there that could jump out and get on anybody that goes by. Now, Jack, I want you to sling off these ditch-banks all the way from the house to town ... both sides.

"Here's you a couple of scythes to work with."

The king brought out two mowing scythes. One of them was brand new and was just as sharp and shiny as it could be. It looked like it had never been used even once. The other one had about a foot broken off of the end of the blade, and there were big gaps out of what blade was left. Both the grips were lost off of the handle of the old scythe.

Jack reached right out and picked up that new mowing scythe. Then he went directly to work.

He would whoosh down a big whoosh of weeds and grass, but, before he could take a step back to whoosh down the next cut, those first ones would jump back up thicker and taller than they ever were to start with. Why, after he came through, there was even grass growing right out into the road where there was no grass at all before!

About lunchtime Jack sat down to rest for a few minutes. Up came the king's daughter to bring him some food to eat.

"What in the world have you been doing, Jack?" she said.

Jack was mad. "I am working hard—can't you see that? I am working so hard that before this day is over this whole road is going to be grown over with weeds and grass! Now, don't you start being smart with me!"

"Jack," she asked, "which mowing scythe do you have?"

"Why, the only one that looked like it would cut anything."

The king's daughter reached in behind her and pulled out that old broken-bladed scythe. She handed it to Jack.

He took one swing with it and it flew out of his hands and started swinging on its own. Every time it would go around it would whoosh down a big cut, and while it was backing up to start over again, another big cut of grass would fall down all on its own. Besides that, all of that cut mess of grass and weeds and nettles fell into piles, just ready to be loaded up and hauled off.

In less than thirty minutes, it was all done. Both sides of the entire road were completely clean.

Jack got the old king and showed him the job. The king shook his head. "I'll swan, Jack! You sure are a worker. Now, tomorrow, I'll really put you onto a job."

That night Jack had a big supper and went right up to bed, because he was really give out after this day of work. Way in the night he felt something pulling on his toe and saying, "Jack, Jack! Wake up!"

Jack opened his eyes a crack, and right there at the foot of his bed stood the king's daughter.

"Now, durn it, Jack!" she fussed at him. "If you want to marry me, then listen. I don't know what in the world my daddy has planned for tomorrow, but whatever it is, if he offers you something old and something new, you *please* take what looks *old*. Now, this time, Jack, do it!"

"All right," said Jack. Then he went right back to sleep again.

The next morning Jack had a big breakfast to get ready for the day. He tried to eat as much as he could because he knew he was going to have to face up to an awful test of some kind. He just didn't know what to expect from the old king next.

Right after breakfast the king took Jack way out to a big old barn where he kept all his horses. "Jack," he started in, "today I'm going to get you to clean out my main horse barn. It is in a terrible mess. Why, it hasn't been cleaned out in so long, it is so deep in there that the horses are even fussing about it.

"Here's a couple of pitchforks for you to use."

The king handed Jack two pitchforks. The first one was brand-new with a long set of sharp, strong tines and a handle so smooth and slick that you could work all day without ever rubbing a blister. The other one was plumb worn out. One of the tines was broken all the way down to a nubbin, and the other tines were worn short and thin. The handle was so rotten and pitted that it didn't look like it would hold the first forkful of manure.

Jack took the new fork and got to work. He waded right in that barn and ended up about up to his knees in manure.

Jack started throwing forkloads of manure out the barn door, but every time he threw one out, the last forkful he had just thrown would hit him in the face as it flew back into the barn all on its own. In fact, most of the time, two piles were flying back into the barn for every one that he threw out.

By about noontime, when Jack sat down to rest, the manure had gotten so deep that Jack's head was bumping the top of the barn on the inside.

About then he heard somebody hollering, "Jack ... Jack! Are you alive in there?" Jack looked up, and there—up on the hill above the barn—stood the king's daughter.

She had brought a sack of food for Jack's lunch, but she stood way back on the hill and held her nose against the smell while she hollered down to Jack.

"What in the world are you trying to do, Jack?"

"Just don't start in on me now," Jack said, feeling put out. "I am working so hard for your daddy that before this day is over there will be manure all the way up into the loft and coming out all the windows."

"Jack, which pitchfork do you have?"

"Why, I have the *new* one, of course. It's the only one that possibly looked like it could have been worth anything."

The king's daughter reached in behind her and pulled out the old, broken pitchfork. She threw it on down there to Jack and said, "Try this one a little bit."

Jack just barely got the first forkful out of his hands when that old pitchfork flew into working all on its own. Old Jack had to stand back out of the way because every time that fork would throw one forkful out the barn door, two or three more piles of manure would fly out all on their own.

In about thirty minutes the whole barn was clean, and most of the manure had flown so far that it had already fertilized a cornfield and a couple of cow pastures.

Jack brought the old king down there and showed him that all the barn mess was cleaned out. "Ah, law, Jack … You sure are some good hand to work. I reckon that you can marry my daughter after all.

"Right after breakfast tomorrow we'll make all the plans and get on with the arrangements."

"Well," Jack sighed. He was so pure tired after this day that all he could do was take a bath and eat supper before he was just falling off to sleep.

Jack did toss and turn around a little during the night that night, but nobody ever did come into his room to disturb him at all during his sleep.

The next morning Jack went right on down to breakfast. He was feeling a lot better now and was looking forward to what was going to unfold on this day.

The old king and the queen both were there, but their daughter wasn't anywhere in sight. Right then Jack started smelling another trick.

The old king looked at Jack and said, "Good morning, Jack. Are you ready to marry my daughter?"

Before Jack could say anything, the king himself hollered out, *"Come on in here, girls!"* With that the door opened and in came not one daughter, but *three!*

The king looked at Jack and said, "Pick out the one you want, and let's get on with it!"

Jack just about died. He looked at all three of them, but he couldn't tell which one was his.

They all three had on heavy shoes, long dresses, and great big overcoats with the collars turned up around their necks. They had big hats pulled way down over their foreheads and scarves wrapped around their faces. Jack couldn't even see their hands because they had gloves on.

The three were all dressed just exactly alike, and Jack just did not know which one to pick.

Then he began to notice a little difference among them. One had on brand-new clothes that didn't look like they had ever been worn before. Why, you could still see the creases where they had been folded up on the shelf.

The next one had on clothes that had seen just a normal amount of wear, neither old nor new.

The last one looked kind of pitiful. She was wearing clothes that were just about clean wore out. They were covered with all kinds of patches and had been mended everywhere.

Jack started rubbing his own thoughts together in his head. Then he said to himself, "If there's one thing I learned around this place, it is that things don't always turn out to be what they look like!"

With that, he reached out and took the gloved hand of the girl who was wearing the worn-out clothes. "This is the one for me!" he said to the king.

She unwrapped her face, and, sure enough, she was the one!

When the others unwrapped, Jack could see that he had done the right thing. The new clothes had been on the oldest daughter, a real mean one, because she always got everything when it was first brand-new.

The regular-worn clothes were on the middle daughter, who was not too bad but not too good either. She always got everything next as hand-me-downs.

That beautiful young daughter that Jack had fallen in love with—she was the king's youngest, and the one he didn't really want Jack to pick, and she never did get anything until it was almost worn out.

So Jack and the king's youngest daughter got married. She was the only one he had ever known about to start with. With half of the treasure in the kingdom they were just as rich as they could be. But people say that Jack turned down getting to be the next king, because he never did much enjoy telling other people what to do.

The Time Jack
Stole the Cows

Jack's encounters with giants did not always end with his disposal of their heads. Sometimes the giants were eliminated by thorough trickery of one sort or another. This story is one I always liked because the giants seemed so nasty and because Jack happened to come up with such good tricks. As usual, in the end, the giants no longer were in the way.

*T*here was one time when Jack was still living with his mama after Tom and Will had already gone off on their own. He was the man of the house now, and this meant that he had to provide food for his mama and himself. Jack was an awful good shot, and he usually didn't have any trouble going hunting and then coming home with something to cook for supper.

One day Jack went off on a long hunting trip, and the farther he went the worse his luck got. He didn't see a single thing to shoot at, and no matter how far he walked, his luck just didn't get any better.

Finally, Jack came to realize that if he didn't start back home fast, he was going to get caught out in the dark for sure before he made it all the way back to his mama. He would have to just try his luck again tomorrow.

He slung his gun over his shoulder and hit it for home, but he had started back too late. In no time it was just as dark as it could possibly be, and Jack couldn't tell a thing about where he was going.

It was in the dark of the moon that night, and besides that it was so cloudy that you couldn't even see any stars to tell your way by. The cloud settled down until Jack was walking in the fog, and he kept falling over roots and rocks and stepping into creeks up to his knees and even walking smack into trees.

He thought, "If I don't find somewhere to hole up and spend the night, I am going to skin all the hide off of my nose before morning." He strained through the dark just trying to make out some sign that would tell him where he was.

Jack came up over the top of a long hill, and right there in a thicket in front of him he could see a light. Boy, was he happy. Here he had come onto somebody's house, though he wasn't close enough yet to tell whose it was. He thought when he got closer and saw where he was he would ask them if he could spend the night.

Jack sure was surprised when he got close up to the house and realized that he had never seen it before. He thought, "It sure *is* dark tonight. Why, I have wandered around in the dark until I have come onto a place I have never been before. I wonder who in the world lives here."

Jack made his way through the fog and the trees on up to the house. He went up the wooden steps and onto the front porch, crossed the porch, and knocked on the door.

Nobody came to the door, and, when Jack knocked again, the door swung about half open. Since no one was at home, it was clear to Jack that the door had been left unlocked by whoever lived there.

Jack stood there and looked in the door. Since the house was not much more than a one-room cabin, he could see about everything there was to see inside. There were three big beds on the back wall, a fireplace at the end, candles burning here and there, and a big table just covered with food.

It looked to Jack like whoever lived there had just been eating and had gone out and left all the food right there on the table. It sure did smell good.

Jack thought, "Whoever these folks are, they must be awful nice and friendly since they don't even lock the door of their house when they leave. I bet they wouldn't mind if I spent the night here with them. I'll just go in and wait for them until they get home."

So Jack went inside the strange house. He stood around for a while until the food smelled so good that he just couldn't stand it. He went over to the table and ate himself a good fill of the leftovers.

After this Jack was so tired that he stretched out on the hearth in front of the fire. In no time he had fallen asleep.

Old Jack slept a pretty long time, and while he slept he had no idea whose house he was in or that they were right at this very time on their way home to where he was asleep.

What Jack didn't know was that he had stumbled into the house of three big giants who had been just terrorizing the whole countryside as robbers. The truth is that they had their house hidden so far back in the woods that they didn't even need to lock the doors, and, lost in the dark, Jack had just stumbled into it.

All of a sudden the door burst open, and the three brother giants were right there in the room with Jack! He popped wide awake and saw the three nastiest brothers he had ever seen.

These three giants were each about fourteen feet tall, and they hadn't brushed their teeth in twenty-seven years. They had green stuff hanging down from between their teeth when they grinned, and they didn't even care because they didn't even have a mama.

The biggest one grabbed Jack by his shirt and shook him in the air.

"Look here," he said, "here's a little old boy who broke into our house to rob us! Why, I think I'll eat him right up right now!"

This big giant had not had a bath in thirty-one years, and the pure smell of him just about made Jack pass out. He opened his mouth up to eat Jack when the next brother broke in.

"Don't eat him; it's not fair," the second brother said. This one had not washed or combed or cut his hair in forty-two years, and it was so long and greasy that it dragged along and made the floor slick. "He's so little that all three of us wouldn't even get a bite ... and ... he's such a clean little thing that he couldn't possibly taste good."

The more wide awake he got, the more scared Jack got. He was sure that his life was just about over. But he pulled his thoughts together and began to try to come up with a plan.

"Now, you boys just wait a minute," he said. "I didn't come to rob you, but I did come here on purpose.

"Boys, I am a *robber* just like you are, and I came here so I could join up with you!" Jack didn't even realize what he was saying. He was just talking as fast as he could trying to slow these nasty giants down from eating him.

"Huh? Huh? Huh?" all three of the big giants said, one after another. "You couldn't be a robber. You're not big enough, and you're not nearly dirty enough."

These giants never did wipe their boots off when they came in the house because they didn't have a mama. So the whole house was as dirty as it could be.

"I am a robber, too," Jack insisted. At least this line was slowing the giants down from eating him, and pretty soon maybe he could think of a way to sneak out of here.

"Well," the dirtiest of the giants said, "if you really are a robber, then you are welcome to join us and stay right here with us. But ... if you are not, then we are going to cut you into three bites and eat you right up without any salt ... even if you are too clean to taste good."

Jack was relieved until he heard what one of the other giants suggested next.

"If you really are a robber, then you won't have any trouble passing a robber test! That's the only fair way to see if you can stay here with us or not." He turned to his brothers and said, "Don't you think so?"

All three of those ugly giants nodded their heads. Jack just stood there and wondered what they were going to think up next.

The biggest one started talking first. "We're hungry, Jack. We were out robbing all night, but we didn't find one single place that had anything decent to eat.

"Why don't you go out and steal us some breakfast, Jack?"

Jack thought that this robber test might not be as hard as he had thought. He thought he might be able to come up with some breakfast if his life really depended upon it.

"I'm in the mood for some roasted cow," the next giant said. "What about if we get him to steal us a cow to roast?" the others agreed.

Now, Jack thought that if he was going to have to steal something, a cow might be the easiest thing he could come up with. After all, all you had to do to steal a cow was go out into a field and lead her out with you. He figured he could do that and still make it up to whoever the cow belonged to when he got home later. He was relieved that this was all there was going to be to the robber test.

Then he heard the rest.

"Jack, there is a farmer who lives on down the road from us," the biggest giant said, giving the full instructions now. "He raises the best roasting cows around. Every morning during this time of the year he takes one of those fat cows into town and sells her at the market.

"What we want you to do to prove that you are a robber like us is to go down to the road and steal that tender roasting cow from that farmer as he leads her to town this morning. Now go, Jack."

When Jack heard this, he didn't know what he was going to do. He had thought that he might be able to steal a cow out of a field with nobody around, but he couldn't figure out how anybody could steal a cow from its owner while he was leading it to town on a rope. But he was going to have to try or he would be the breakfast instead of the cow.

Jack started out down toward the road where the farmer was supposed to come by, all the while trying to figure out what he was going to do when he got there.

On the way, he happened to pass a place where two other farmers were butchering a hog. They had the dead hog strung up, had already scalded it to scrape off the hair, and were just starting to clean out the insides. Jack had helped his daddy do this when his daddy was still living, and he thought about that when he saw this hog.

Then he had an idea. He walked over to where the hog-butchering was going on and asked the farmers, "Could you let me have this hog's bladder?"

They said, "Sure, Jack," and gave him the bladder. They figured that Jack wanted to blow the bladder up and make a kicking ball out of it. But Jack wanted the bladder because he knew that it would be full of blood.

Jack took the bladder of blood, thanked the farmers, and went on down to the road where the farmer with the cow was supposed to come.

Once he got there, he got ready. He messed up his hair and wrinkled up his clothes. He rubbed dirt on his face and threw dirt all over his clothes and in his hair. Then he poked a hole in that hog's bladder with his knife and dribbled the hog's blood all over him everywhere.

After that, Jack rolled around in the dirt a little more, then lay out real still on his back in the middle of the road. He looked just like he was dead.

Pretty soon here came the farmer on his way to town.

He rounded the curve of the road just below where Jack was, and, all of a sudden, he spotted Jack.

"O Lord!" he hollered. "There is a *dead* boy! I'd better run and get the sheriff and bring him on up here to see this!" The farmer tied the rope of the cow to a tree, told her that he would be right back, and started running to town to get the sheriff.

As soon as he was out of sight, the "dead boy" got up, untied the cow, and led her straight up there to the robbers' house.

The three robbers were tickled to death! "Good boy, Jack. Now you can eat with us." They cut the cow into four pieces and roasted it in the fireplace. They each ate their pieces, hide and bones and all, but Jack only picked at his.

When the giants noticed how dirty and bloody and beat-up Jack was, they said, "Lord, Jack. You look like you had an awful fight getting this cow."

"It was a job," Jack answered them with a smile. "But I'll tell you this. This is not one drop of my own blood that I ended up coming home with. I came out on top!"

Those giants were sure enough impressed with Jack by now.

"Well, boys," he asked the giants, "did I pass the robber test?"

"You sure did, Jack," all the robbers said, still chewing while they talked. "This is just a fine cow for breakfast. You can indeed stay right here with us and be another robber like we are."

"That's good," Jack said, "but I have just a little business to do with my mama. I need to go home for a little while."

"Not so fast, Jack," the biggest robber said. "You've only passed one part of the robber test. You know that all of these tests like this have three parts. You've got to pass the other parts before we can trust you to go far out of our sight."

Jack was heartbroken, but there seemed to be no getting away. "What's the next part of the test?" he asked, wanting to get on with it.

The giants thought a minute; then one of then said, "Jack, that roasted cow was so good that I think we ought to have another one for our breakfast tomorrow.

"What you are going to have to do next is to go down there in the morning and steal the next cow that farmer brings to town. Do that, Jack, and you'll be two-thirds finished!"

Jack didn't have any choice. He spent the night there with never a chance to slip out, and, the next morning, he started back down to the road to steal another cow.

Jack was pretty sure that the dead-boy trick wouldn't work two days in a row. So he was pacing back and forth in the road just trying to think up something to do to get another cow.

While he was pacing there, he spotted a woman's shoe lying right over by the side of the road. He picked it up.

There the shoe was—nearly new, Jack thought. He figured that somebody must have dropped it on their way home from town. It maybe never had even been worn. Jack wondered if the other shoe of the pair might be around somewhere.

He looked all up and down the sides of the road, but there was no other shoe to be found. Evidently the loser of the shoe had just dropped one out of the pair.

Then he had an idea.

Jack wiped all the dust off of the shoe until it was right shiny. Then he put it right smack in the middle of the road and hid in the woods so he could watch when the farmer came.

In a few minutes here the farmer came around the curve in the road, pulling the cow by the rope.

All of a sudden the farmer spotted the shoe. He stopped short, then picked it up.

"Why, look here," the farmer said to himself. "Somebody has lost a shoe. I wonder who it was." The farmer looked inside the shoe to see its size.

"It's a size thirteen … just right for my wife! I wonder if the mate to it is around here somewhere."

With that, the farmer started searching the roadsides for the other shoe, with no more luck than Jack had had. Finally, he threw the shoe back down in the road right near where he had picked it up to begin with.

"I reckon there's just one. One shoe won't do anybody any good. I might as well get shut of it." Then the farmer and his cow started walking on down the road toward town.

As soon as the farmer was out of sight, Jack popped out of his hiding place and picked up the shoe. He took off carrying it as he ran up a shortcut that led over the top of the mountain and came down on the other side.

By taking the shortcut, Jack came out in the very road to town that the farmer was following, except that he got there long before the farmer did.

Jack took that very same shoe that the farmer had looked at on the other side of the mountain, dusted it off again, and put it right there in the very middle of the road. Again he hid in the woods and waited for the farmer to arrive with his cow.

Before long the farmer got there. He rounded the last curve in the road and then spotted the shoe.

"Law, me!" he said. "There's the other shoe!" He picked it up and checked the size just to be sure. Sure enough, it was a size thirteen just like the first one.

"I'll go back and get the first one, and I can take both of them home to my wife. Boy, will she like this!"

With that, the farmer tied the cow to a tree and took off back down the road to get the first shoe.

As soon as he was out of sight, Jack popped out of the woods, untied that cow, and led her straight back to the giants' house.

The three giants had been waiting for a long time, and they were awful hungry. "We didn't think you were going to do it, Jack. But you did!"

"I sure did," Jack said proudly, "and today I didn't even get messed up. This is getting easier all the time."

The giants whacked the cow up, roasted her, and ate every bite. Jack ate all he could of his part, and then they finished even the horns and hooves that he left behind.

Finally Jack said, "Boys, I'd better go home and check on my mama. She will be awful worried about me since I haven't been home in a day or two."

"No, Jack," the biggest giant spoke for all of them. "You are only two-thirds through the test. You have to pass the last bit before we can trust you to leave." Jack had no choice but to stay there for another day.

Early the next morning the giants were up and waiting for Jack to get his clothes on.

"We are hungry again, Jack." It was the youngest one who was doing the talking this time. "We want you just to go back down there and steal us another roasting cow to eat. That can be the rest of your robbing test."

So, not having any idea at all about what he was going to do this time, Jack started out down to the road for the third time.

He was thinking to himself as hard as he could. "The dead boy trick will just not work again ... the shoe trick will never work again ... what am I going to do? What am I going to do?"

Jack was about to despair of an idea when he heard the farmer and the cow coming right up the road toward where he was. He could hear the farmer begging the cow, "Come on, Bossy," and he could hear the cow complaining, "MOOooo, MMooOOO!" When he heard the cow, Jack knew what he was going to do.

He climbed right up the bank of the hill above the road, hid in a thicket of laurel bushes, and waited for the farmer and the cow to get close.

When they were right below him, the farmer jerked the cow's rope and the cow went, "Mmooooo!" When Jack heard that, he grabbed one of the laurel bushes and shook it real hard and went, "MmmooOOOO!" right back at the cow.

The farmer said, "What was that?"

Jack shook the laurel bush again and bellowed, "MMmoOO ... mmmOOO!"

With that, the farmer almost laughed out loud. "Why," he said to himself, "that's one of my lost cows! I *knew* that they had pulled loose from where I tied them and just wandered off. That's one of them, and I'll bet you that the other one's around here somewhere, too!"

By that time Jack had worked his way around the hillside until he was in a clump of blueberry bushes. He rattled the blueberry bushes and let out, "mmMMMOOO!"

Now the farmer yelled, "There's the other one!" Then he turned to the cow on the end of his rope and said, "Now, Bossy, you stay right here while I go round up your sisters." He tied that third cow to a little bush while he followed the mooing sound up the hillside to get his two lost cows.

Jack scrambled on around the hillside, mooing as he went, until he had the farmer way up above the road. Then he scooted down the hill under the bushes, untied that third cow, and took her straight back to the giants' house.

"Here is number three!" he announced to them.

The three giants were so tickled that they danced around. They whacked this cow up, roasted and ate her right up. Jack ate as much of his part as he could. He knew he was going to get to leave now.

"You are a robber, Jack," the oldest giant spoke for the others. "We want you to stay right here and live with us from now on!"

"Well," Jack said, "that is a fine idea. But first, I want to prove something else to you."

"What's that?" all three giants asked. "You already passed the robber test."

"I know that," Jack went on. "But, fellers, I just stole the things you asked me to steal.

"I want to show you how much stuff I can steal on my own."

"What do you like to steal?" they asked.

Jack looked around their house. "Oh," he kept on, "the kind of stuff you have gathered up here … Why, I'll bet you that in *one hour* I can steal *on my own* as much stuff as all three of you have stolen and brought into this house *in one year!*"

The giants were amazed. They couldn't believe that one little boy could possible steal as much as they had in a year. So they said, "We will wait right here, Jack. Go to it. We want to see what you come up with."

Jack took off and headed as straight as he could to the sheriff's house.

Once he found the sheriff, he asked him, "Have you been having any trouble with robbers around here?"

"Law, yes!" the sheriff answered him. "People have been having everything they own stolen, and a few of them have said that they've seen *giants* carrying it off. But we can't keep up to follow them or know where they live or hide out. What do you know about this?"

"Well, Sheriff," Jack's plan went on, "what would you give if you could find those giant robbers and catch them?"

"Oh, Jack," the sheriff offered, "we would give you half of everything that they have stolen as a reward just for getting rid of them. That would surely be worth it."

"Come on, Sheriff," Jack motioned. They took off straight back to the giants' house.

When they got there, Jack and the sheriff and his men surrounded the house. Then they jumped in the door and tied the giants up before they knew what got them. All three of them were put under arrest right on the spot!

The giants had a fit. "Jack," the oldest one said, "you lied to us! You said you were going out to steal more stuff than we could steal and look what you did. You got the sheriff! That's not stealing anything!"

"Oh, boys," Jack smiled at the giants, "you just don't know what stealing is." Jack looked at the sheriff. "Tell them about my reward, Sheriff!"

And so the sheriff told the giants that, for helping to get them caught, Jack got to keep half of all the stuff the three of them had stolen. Then they figured out that Jack did indeed get more stuff in one hour than all three of them had managed to get in the last year.

After the giants were taken off to prison, Jack brought his mama up there to live with him in the giants' house. After they cleaned it up and aired it out, it was as fine a place to live as you ever saw. And, with everything they had as Jack's reward, they had enough stuff to sell and trade on for food for a right long time.

The Time Jack Helped the King Catch His Girls

In almost every story I ever heard about Jack, when a king's daughter was involved, he ended up marrying her in the end. The following is the one story in which Jack turned down part of the reward. I have later learned other Western European versions of this story theme. Here, I try to tell it they way I heard it before I ever met the Grimm Brothers.

There was another time when old Jack left his mama and went out on his own just to try to seek his fortune. He had been wandering around and about for a pretty long time, and he was getting low on food to eat and money to buy more with. Jack was getting anxious to stumble onto about any kind of job or deal that might keep him from starving to death.

But, no matter how hard he kept on the lookout, Jack just didn't have any kind of luck at all. Finally he got down to his last quarter, and, since he hadn't found any work in the town he was in, he decided to quit it and try his luck in the next town along the way.

He bought a fresh loaf of bread with his last few cents of money and started out on his way.

Jack walked all of one day, and still he was having no luck at all finding a new way to make a living. He ate about a fourth of his loaf of bread on this first day and saved the rest for later. On the next two days he still had no luck, and by the fourth day he was down to his last bread, with no money at all and getting desperate for some luck.

Jack was about to starve clean to death that morning, but he could just not bring himself to eat up that last little bit of bread. He would hold out as long as he could.

Jack didn't see anybody for a long time that day, and then, way up in the morning he met a scrawny, poor-looking old woman. She was coming along the road with her shawl drawn up tight around her shoulders.

"Good morning, sonny!" the old woman said.

"Good morning to you," Jack replied. "Where are you going on a day like this?"

The old woman looked straight at Jack and said, "I'm out seeking my fortune."

"Well, so am I!" Jack fairly exclaimed. "Have you had any luck?"

"Not at all," the old woman answered. "I have run clean out of money and food both. You wouldn't have a little something I could have to eat, would you?"

Jack thought to himself, "I've only got a fourth of a loaf of bread standing between myself and pure starvation. Still, I don't feel right keeping it to myself when somebody else is hungry."

So he said to the old woman, "I sure do! I've got a right good chunk of bread. Why don't we just sit down right here and share it half and half."

Jack and the old woman sat down on a log under a big oak tree, and they both started eating that last piece of bread. The woman tore into that bread like she was starved to death. Jack couldn't eat his bread, he was watching her gobble so.

Then he began to notice something else. With every bite of bread that the old woman took, she looked different. She seemed to get younger and younger all the time until, by the time she finished eating, she was about the same age as Jack himself.

Jack couldn't believe what he was seeing. "Bedads!" he fairly hollered. "You must be some kind of magic!"

"You could say that, Jack. And all day long I've been looking for somebody to share my magic with. I needed something to work with, though.

"All day long I have been asking people if they would share just a little food with me, and, Jack, I have met people who had so much that they couldn't carry it all. But do you know, not one person would share anything with me until I met you.

"You had less than anybody else, Jack, but you gave me what you had. And, Jack, I'm going to share some of my magic with you in case you need it along the way."

"Oh," Jack said shyly, "you don't have to do that."

"I know, Jack. That's part of why I want to do it."

The old woman, who now looked young, reached way down into a leather pack that she had. She felt around and then began coming up with things that she started handing to Jack.

First she handed him what looked like a dry, rolled-up laurel leaf. "Take this with you, Jack. When you come to water that you need to cross, drop it in the water and it will carry you across. All you have to do is to tell it where to take you."

Next she pulled out a hat that looked just like the kind of knit wool toboggan that his mama used to make for him and his brothers. "This, Jack, is a sleepy-wakey cap. If you need to sleep, just put it on right-side-out. Then you can sleep through anything. But if you need to stay awake, then put it on *inside-out*. That way it'll keep you awake, no matter what!

Jack couldn't say anything. He had never seen or heard of anything like this. He just waited to see what she was going to come up with next.

The woman had an old, worn-out-looking cloak that she was not wearing but was carrying slung over her shoulder. She untied it and held it out to Jack.

"Oh, you can't give me your coat," he objected.

"I don't need it to keep warm, Jack. I can keep warm just fine. You don't need it to keep warm either. This is a cloak with a different purpose."

Jack watched while the woman unfolded the cloak and wrapped it around her shoulders. Just as she drew the cloak together in front, she vanished into thin air! "Jack," she was saying all right, though he couldn't see a thing, "this is an invisible cloak. Just put it over yourself, or anything else for that matter, and nobody will be able to see a thing. It won't hurt you a bit, though."

Jack said, "I've sure never seen anything like that," as the woman took the cloak off and reappeared again.

"Nobody has, Jack!" she laughed. "Now, thank you for the bread, *and* good luck with your fortune." Then she disappeared.

Jack put the leaf-boat in his pocket. He put the cap and the cloak in his packsack and started out on his way.

Late in the afternoon, he came to a ford in the river where the road went through the water and on across to the other side. Jack didn't want to have to get wet, but there weren't any boats and no way to get across but to wade through the water.

He thought to himself, "I'll just wait here until somebody comes along in a wagon or on a horse. Then I can hitch a ride across to the other side and not get wet." Jack waited and waited, but nobody ever did come along.

After a while Jack stood up and shoved both hands down into his pockets. He was tired of waiting. When his hands went into his pockets, Jack felt that laurel leaf that the woman had given him. "I just think I'll try this thing out," he said to himself.

Jack walked down to the edge of the stream and dropped the leaf in the shallow part. When it hit the water it started unrolling and swelling until, in about half a minute, it had turned into a little boat. The boat was about the size of an Indian canoe and looked just right for one person.

Jack got in. He thought out loud, "Now, how do I get this thing to go over to the other side?" Just as soon as he heard himself say that, the boat took off and carried Jack right over to the other side of that river in no time at all.

He pulled the little boat out of the stream. As the water dripped off, the boat started shrinking and shrinking until it was just like a little curled-up laurel leaf again.

Jack put the leaf in his pocket and smiled to himself as he walked along the road to the next town. There he was able to work out a meal and a place to spend the night in exchange for splitting a big pile of wood at a little inn in the town. He split the wood, ate supper, and went up to bed.

He was plumb give out after walking all day and then splitting wood after that, and Jack had an awful time settling down to sleep. On top of that, a big bunch of heavy drinkers had come into the inn just at Jack's bedtime. They were singing and hollering and throwing furniture around until Jack just couldn't get to sleep at all.

"I wonder," Jack thought. He reached inside his pack and pulled out that sleepy-wakey cap. He checked to be sure it was right-side-out, then put it on.

The next thing Jack knew, it was the middle of the next morning. Birds were singing, the sun was way up, and he felt just as rested as he could be.

Jack got up and packed all of his stuff. He thanked the keeper of the inn for the place to stay and the food; then he went on toward the next town, still seeking his fortune.

Jack didn't have one single thing with him that he could eat this day. By the middle of the day he was fairly starving.

The road through that part of the country was running alongside a fairly nice farm. As he kept walking, Jack came to a fenced-in field, and out in this field stood an old rock chimney, marking the site where an old house had once been. All around this old house place were apple trees full of apples.

Jack climbed over the fence and started over toward where he knew he could get a few of the apples, when all of a sudden he saw a big red bull coming right at him out of the trees. He turned and ran as hard as a hungry boy could run and fairly flew over that fence just in time to escape the bull. The old red bull just stood there on the other side of the fence, stomping and snorting.

Jack was so disappointed. He was just terribly hungry.

"I wonder," he thought to himself. Then he pulled that old cloak out of his packsack and put it around his shoulders. All of a sudden the old red bull started looking around and around like he had lost something.

Right over the fence slipped old Jack. The bull just looked right toward him but couldn't see a thing. Jack was just as invisible as he could possibly be. He went right up to those apple trees and picked up all he could carry under his cloak; then he walked right by that bull and climbed back out over the fence.

When he took off the cloak, the bull saw him standing there with all of those apples. That old bull snorted and pawed up the ground, then just gave up and ran on off. Jack ate a couple of those apples, put the rest in his packsack, and went on his way to the next town.

Just about as soon as he got into town, Jack saw all the loose people in the whole place gathered around a big tree and looking at a sign that had been nailed up there.

The sign said: REWARD OFFERED ... WAGONLOAD OF GOLD AND DAUGHTER IN MARRIAGE TO WHOEVER CAN SOLVE THE KING'S MYSTERY.

Jack read the sign along with everybody else. Then he turned and asked the man standing beside him, "What's the king's mystery?"

"Don't you know?" the man questioned Jack right back. "You must not be from around here." Then he went on to explain it to Jack.

"The old king has three of the prettiest daughters in the world, but there is something going on with them that he can't understand.

"Every night all three of them are slipping out. Then they are right back in their room in the morning where they are supposed to be. The king can't figure out where they go, or how they get out or back in. But they can manage to get out no matter if he locks up every single door in the house!

"Anybody who can help him figure out what is going on up there gets a whole wagonload of gold *and* gets to marry whichever one of the daughters he wants to get married to."

"This is just what I've been looking for," Jack said.

"Now, son, you be careful," the man told him. "You just get three nights to figure it out, and if you fail, the old king will just throw you right in the swamp and you'll never come back!"

"I'm not scared of that," Jack smiled back at him.

And so Jack, without waiting around to hear anything else, went right on up to the king's castle. He knocked right on the door until the old king himself came right out there and answered the door.

"Hello, King. I'm Jack. I have come all the way here just to solve your big mystery!"

"Do you know about the swamp?" the king asked Jack. "There's all kinds of snakes and awful varmints waiting in there to get you if you fail. Are you sure you want to try?"

"I know all about all of that stuff, and I am not afraid," Jack bragged to him.

So the king invited Jack on inside the castle house. They ate a big supper together with all three of the daughters and the old queen herself. Jack had a hard time swallowing his food because those three girls were so pretty they made his adam's apple jump around all over the place.

After supper the girls went up to their room. Then the king set in to tell Jack everything about the big mystery.

"It all began getting my attention," the king started, "when my three girls got harder and harder to get up out of bed in the mornings. Then they started just lying around all day like they didn't have any energy at all. It just seemed to me like they had been up all night.

"So," the king went on with his story, "one night I slipped up and peeked in their bedroom when they were supposed to be sound asleep. They were gone! I tried to stay up there and watch for them to come back in, but I fell asleep. When I woke up, they were back, right there in their beds asleep. I just couldn't figure it out.

"Now, Jack, I can send them up to bed and lock all of the doors and windows, and still they somehow get out and then back in without ever getting caught. It's way too high up for them to climb in and out through the window, but they are going and coming somehow.

"The mystery," the king almost whispered in Jack's ear now, "is to find out how they are getting out and where they go when they are out there. If you can solve that, I will gladly give you a wagonful of gold. Besides that, solve the question and you can pick out whichever one of those girls you would like and marry her.

"This is the deal, Jack. You get three nights to try ... then it's into the swamp! Are you up for it, Jack?"

"Don't you worry about me," Jack said. "You just give me a room to sleep in that is pretty close to theirs, and I will see what I can do."

With that, the king took Jack upstairs and put him in the room that was straight across the hall from the girls' room. Jack got ready to go to bed; then he heard a knock at his door.

When he opened his door, all three of those girls stood there. They held out a mugful of hot, spicy cider to Jack, and the oldest one said, "We just brought you something nice to drink, Jack. Have a good night's sleep!" They left.

Jack didn't know that they had made up a sleepy drink and brought it to him, just like the one they mixed up for their daddy every night. It didn't make any difference, though, because before he took a sip, he got out his sleepy-wakey cap, turned it *inside-out,* and put it on to keep him awake. After that he drank the sleepy cider, but with the cap on he stayed wide awake.

Just as the clock struck midnight, Jack saw a flicker of light under their door. Someone in there had just lit a candle. Right quick he put on his invisible cloak and slipped over toward their door.

Jack didn't know how he was going to get into their room without their seeing the door open. He didn't have to worry, though, because one of them opened the door, just to look out and be sure nobody was watching out in the hall. While she was peeking up and down the hall, Jack, just as invisible as he could be, slipped past her and was right inside their room.

All three of the girls were all dressed up, just like for a party. All of a sudden all three of them stepped up on the bed that was in the middle. The one in front knocked three knocks on the headboard of that bed, *and* that headboard itself swung open just like a door! Behind it Jack could see a dark, low passageway leading right into the wall.

The three girls stepped through the opening, and Jack, still invisible, went right through there behind them.

The passageway was dark, except for the one candle the oldest of the girls was carrying. The way sloped down and down and wound around and around as well as back and forth. Sometimes it was so steep that there would be a set of steps to make it easier to go down.

Finally they seemed to come out in a big, open cavern. It was so big and dark in there that you couldn't see either the top or the other side.

"We must be way down inside the earth," Jack thought. He could hear water lapping nearby. He followed the three girls toward the sound of the water, and, all of a sudden, they were at a built-up rock boat-dock beside an underground lake that just disappeared off into the dark and fog.

The girl with the candle reached in a little hollow in the rocks and pulled out a cow's horn. She blew on that horn real loud three times.

In a minute Jack could see a light, like the light from a lantern, bobbing up and down out over the water. As the light came closer, he could see that it was a lantern riding in the bow of a boat. That boat was being rowed by somebody whose coat was so big and floppy that Jack couldn't see if it was a man or a woman.

The boat came right up to the dock, and the three girls stepped down into it. There was plenty of room for Jack, but he was just too scared to step in there. In a second, the boat was gone.

Then Jack remembered the laurel-leaf boat in his pocket! He felt for it and pulled it out. As soon as Jack dropped the leaf into the water, it started swelling up into that same little boat he had used before. Jack stepped right in. He noticed that if he spread his invisible cloak out over the sides of the boat, the boat was invisible, too.

"I wonder where that other boat went," Jack said out loud. Of course, as soon as he said this, his boat started out through the dark until in no time Jack could see the bobbing light of the lantern in the boat with the girls. Soon he was following right behind them, but they couldn't see him at all. In fact, it even made Jack himself feel a little funny to be gliding over the water without being able to see a boat under him.

Pretty soon Jack saw more and more lights up ahead. There was a pier coming out into the water and a lot of lights running along the shore. The girls' boat pulled up and stopped, and they all got out. They stood there for a few minutes like they were waiting for somebody. This was a good thing because it gave time for Jack to pull his boat out of the water so it could shrink up and go back into his pocket.

Jack heard hoof sounds and then saw a carriage pulled by a team of gray horses. The girls got in, and Jack jumped right up on the trunk rack on the back end of the carriage and rode along with them. He never did get a chance to look at the driver.

When the carriage stopped and Jack got off, they were in front of a big, beautiful castle. It was all lit up, and he could smell food and hear music. Three fine-looking young men came out to the carriage and took the three girls inside.

Jack had never spent a night like this before in his life. Being invisible, he could check everything out as much as he wanted to. That party went on for four or five hours with lots of dancing and drinking and eating and all sorts of carrying on. Jack thought, "The old king will never believe this!" So he slipped a silver candleholder under his invisible cloak to take back to show to the king.

Pretty soon everybody started home. The young men kissed the three girls a lot, and then the girls and Jack hopped the carriage for a ride back to the boat.

They got back home just exactly the same way they went. Once in their room, they put up their party clothes and put on their nightgowns. All three girls fell asleep just about at the same time as the sun came up.

Poor old Jack was worn out! He went back into his room, took off the sleepy-wakey cap, and fell asleep until it was time to eat dinner. Then he went down to see the king.

Jack sat down with the king and told him the whole story, including all about his sleepy-wakey cap, his invisible robe, and his laurel-leaf boat. He told the king about the head of the bed being a door, the underground lake, and all about the big party.

"Why, that is the all-overest big tale that I have ever heard!" laughed the king. "Do you think that I would believe such a made-up bunch of stuff as that? Jack, I could make up a better story than that myself and have it sound more like the truth. I ought to throw you in the swamp right now!"

"Now wait!" Jack about cried out. "I've brought something from the party to prove it was real." Jack pulled out the silver candleholder and handed it to the king.

"There it is!" the king hollered out. "This is the very candlestick that disappeared from this very table last week. Yes, it looks just like it. Jack, I ought to throw you in the swamp right now."

Jack was so mixed up by all of this that he didn't know what to think or do. "Just you wait," he mumbled. "I'm supposed to get two more chances."

"Oh, all right," grumbled the king.

Jack ate some lunch; then he went back on up to his room to sleep for a while to get ready for his next long night.

At suppertime, there were the girls, looking just like they had just got up out of bed. They all wanted to know if Jack had slept all right during the night before. He told them that he got along through the night just fine.

After supper they all sat around and talked for a while. Then the girls said they were tired, and everybody went up to bed.

Jack went in his own room, but in just a minute there was a knock at the door. The girls came in. "We brought you a better pillow," one of them said. "That old pillow that's in here is so lumpy that nobody could sleep on it."

"Why, thanks," Jack said. "I sure could use that."

Since Jack had put on his sleepy-wakey cap wrong-side-out before he got in the bed, he never did even know that the pillow they brought was a sleepy pillow, the very kind they fluffed up to keep the queen asleep every night. That cap kept him awake no matter what kind of pillow he had.

At midnight he lit out for their room. They didn't even check the hall this time, so Jack had to slip in the door of their room while they had their backs turned to knock on that bed. He had to fly to get himself and his invisible cloak through that door before the headboard slammed shut.

Everything happened just exactly the same way that it had happened the night before. This night, while Jack was observing the goings-on at the party in the strange underground castle, he was determined to take something back to really prove his story to the king.

Jack was keeping his eyes on a big silver punchbowl. When it was nearly empty and the servant taking care of it went in the kitchen to bring more punch, Jack slipped that whole big silver punchbowl under his invisible cloak.

He had an awful time getting back with that big thing! Jack about got caught in the castle door; he nearly fell off the trunk rack on the carriage; he almost turned over in his little boat; and he just about didn't make it out through that headboard door.

Finally Jack was back in his own room with the silver punchbowl. He was really proud that he had brought back something that would really prove his story to the king.

This morning Jack didn't even need his sleepy-wakey cap to help him sleep for a while. He was plumb give out. Like before, he slept until the middle of the day, then went down to meet the king for something to eat.

"Well, Jack, do you have another big tale to tell me for today?"

Jack told him the whole story all over again.

"That is pitiful, Jack," the king said. "At least you could have told me a new lie instead of trying the same old one again."

"Just you wait," Jack said, really annoyed now. "This time I have brought something to show you that you can't just laugh about."

"Well, it better not be a silver punchbowl," the king growled. "The cook says that somebody slipped in and stole our very best one last week!"

Jack didn't say a thing. Then he finally said to the king, "At least I have one more night to try."

That afternoon Jack didn't sleep. He spent the whole rest of the day trying to think of what he could do to prove his story to the king. Finally it came to him.

Jack wrapped his invisible cloak around him and slipped down to the king's sitting room. It was still way before supper-time, and the king was just sitting there all alone and thinking to himself.

Jack just watched the king for a few minutes, trying to decide exactly how to impress him the most.

It was cool in the room, and as Jack watched, the king got up and started to build a fire. Jack slipped up to where he was putting wood in the fireplace. Every time the king would put a stick of wood in the fireplace, Jack would take it out and toss it across the room!

The old king was fairly sweating to figure out how that wood was bouncing right back out of the fireplace.

Jack laughed and then popped right out of the invisible cloak right in front of the king. The old king nearly fainted! Then Jack showed the king the invisible cloak and how it worked. After this the king decided that maybe this Jack did have a little something to pay attention to after all.

After seeing this little show, the king was ready to listen when Jack explained his plan for the night. Using the sleepy-wakey cap, the invisible cloak, and the laurel-leaf boat, Jack was going to send the king himself after the girls so he could see everything for himself

The king agreed. After supper he pretended to be going up to his own room to bed, but instead he went up to Jack's room and hid under Jack's bed.

Pretty soon the girls went to their room, and Jack went to his. He told the king to stay hidden under the bed a little longer.

Sure enough, in a few minutes there was a knock at Jack's door. He opened it, and there stood the girls with a big quilt. "It's going to get awful cold tonight, Jack. We thought you might need this to keep warm." Jack didn't know that this was a sleepy quilt, just sprinkled all over with sleepy powder.

Jack took the quilt and shut the door. "Come on out," he said to the king. "It's time for you to get ready."

Then Jack showed the king how to turn the sleepy-wakey cap wrong-side-out and wear it that way to stay awake. He gave the king the invisible cloak which the king already knew how to operate. Finally he gave the king the little laurel-leaf boat.

"You'll just have to trust me that this thing works," Jack told him. "Just remember, this boat is a lot of the reason that I never was scared of getting thrown in your old swamp."

The king got all wide-awake and ready. Jack got in the bed and pulled the sleepy-quilt over him. He was about due for a good night's rest.

At the stroke of midnight, the king saw a flicker of light under the girls' door and was on his way. He slipped into their room and saw that, sure enough, they were all dressed up.

The king followed them right up on the middle of the bed, and, *tap-tap-tap,* that doorway opened. He followed them right through the headboard door, down and down to the big underground lake, and on to the party castle.

Everything happened just exactly the way that Jack had said it would. Jack had described it all so well that the old king almost thought that he had been there before.

When the party was over, the king followed them right on back home to their own room. Then he ran quickly across to Jack's room just in time for the sun to come up.

Jack sure was relieved to hear the old king's story! Boat or no boat, he didn't want to get thrown in the swamp, and he did want that wagonload of gold. But now he wanted more than ever for the king to believe what he had been trying to tell him.

"What do we do next?" he asked the king.

"You just wait until dinnertime," the king answered.

Of course the girls slept all day as usual. Finally, at dinnertime, the king, Jack, and the girls were all together.

"I want to tell you girls something," the king said. He then commenced to tell the three girls the whole story about how Jack had found out the answer to the whole mystery. They all turned awful red in the face when they heard all of this.

"What do you say about that?" the king asked his daughters. They couldn't do anything but confess that it was all true. They cried and cried because they had been caught at last.

The king turned toward Jack. "Well, Jack," he said, "it's time for your reward." He had Jack look out the window, and right outside was a great big wagon just running over with sacks of gold coins. Jack was just as pleased as he could be.

"Now," said the king, "now for the rest of your reward. Jack, which one of these girls do you want to marry? Take your own choice and she will be yours."

Jack thought for a minute, but not for long. "I don't want to marry any of them!" he said.

"None of them?" the king asked. "Why, they are the most beautiful girls in all the world!"

"I can see that," Jack said. "But, King," he went on, "all three of them have spent more time and energy on trying to fool you than they have on anything else. I'd just as soon not get hitched up with anybody like that!"

The old king sure did understood this. He slapped Jack on the back and laughed. Then he gave him the wagon and the four good horses to keep after he pulled his load of gold home with them.

This was the one time that Jack made a fortune without getting married.

The Time Jack
Got the Wishing Ring

Almost always Jack gets himself out of a mess by the use of his wits or the special gifts he receives. This story, which includes some scenery that was very interesting to me as a child, ends very abruptly when Jack makes use of a forgotten gift. I remember it as a good boy's story.

There was one time when Jack and Tom and Will were living with their daddy and their mama.

All three of them were getting anxious to get out on their own and to go look for their fortunes. They were getting pretty well grown up by now.

One day Jack's daddy came to them and told about the plan he had to offer them. "Boys," he started, "I have bought some land up on the other side of the mountain from here. If you boys want, it can just be yours. Then you can go on up there and try your hand at farming and making your own living the way you've been talking about doing.

"What do you think about that?"

Jack and Tom and Will thought it was just fine. It seemed to them like it was just exactly the chance they had been waiting for.

So they loaded up a few tools that their daddy knew they would need; they loaded up some pots and pans their mama picked out for them; and they loaded up their clothes and some groceries. Then their daddy took them over to where the land was by hauling all of their things in the ox cart and on a little mule he gave them to work their new land with.

Once there, he put them out and left them there to make do on their own.

They just had a great time. It was the spring of the year, and the weather was just fine. In just a few days those three brothers had built themselves a little log house out of poplar logs and had cleared a newground with the little mule their daddy had left with them. It was just the right time of the year to put crops in, and they were going to fend for themselves very well.

Each day one of the three boys took a turn at cooking while the other two went out to plant and to clear more newground. That way they really couldn't fuss about the food since whoever fussed was soon going to have his turn at cooking.

One day it was Tom's turn to cook. Will and Jack left him at home to work on dinner, and the two of them and the mule headed on off to work at being farmers for the day.

Once they were gone, Tom started on the cooking. He boiled up a big pot of dried beans and baked a big oven full of cornbread. It sure did smell good.

About the time it was all done, he went out the door and beat on a piece of a railroad rail they had tied up there to make a dinner bell. This was the way they called each other to eat every day when the time was right.

Tom looked down the road, and, instead of Jack and Will, he saw a great big old giant of a man with a long blue beard that hung down so far it was dragging beside him on the ground. This man was huge and looked mean. Just the sight of him scared

Tom so badly that he ran and hid under the bed, but he forgot to shut and lock the front door.

That big blue-bearded man came right on in the front door of their house, walked over to the stove, and ate the whole pot of beans and the entire cake of cornbread. Then he left by the same way he had come and was plumb gone by the time Jack and Will got up to the house.

Jack and Will came in the door, and Tom was still hiding under the bed. He crawled out from under the bed when he heard that it was Will and Jack in the house. Then he told them about what had happened with the old blue-bearded man.

"That is just a big lie!" Will said right back to him. "I know what the truth is ... you just didn't want to cook anything for dinner. So, instead of cooking, you just made up that big tale about the blue-bearded man."

Jack agreed with everything Will thought and said.

Poor old Tom didn't have a chance at getting anybody to believe his story. Both of his brothers were against him. All three of them had to go without dinner until they all scrounged up some leftovers and made a cold meal of it.

"You just wait until tomorrow, Will!" Tom told him. "I hope that giant of a man comes back and just scares you to death. Then you'll believe what I'm telling you."

The next day it was Will's turn to stay home and cook while Jack and Tom worked at the newground. They said they would see him at dinnertime and took off.

Will was determined to make a real meal for them all today. He sliced off some pieces of ham and fried them out. He cooked a pot of spring creasy-greens and made a pan of biscuits to eat with the red-eye gravy from the ham. This was going to be a fine dinner.

When the biscuits were almost done, Will went out the door and went to ringing on that old railroad-rail bell to call his brothers to come and eat. He whanged on it hard and made a big racket.

Will looked down the road, and, instead of his brothers, he saw coming there a great big old blue-bearded man. His beard was dragging the ground, and he looked to Will like he was twice the size of an ordinary human being.

Will didn't even have time to think about how Tom had been telling the truth. No, he was so scared that without even thinking about anything he ran back in the house and hid right back under the bed.

Sure enough, that old blue-bearded man came right on up in the house and ate up the ham, the greens, the biscuits and all of the red-eye gravy. Then he left back out of there exactly the same way he had come.

Will was still way back under the bed when Tom and Jack came in the house. When Tom saw that there wasn't any food, he went over and looked under the bed to find Will. He already knew what had happened.

Jack still didn't believe it. "Both of you are fooling me!" he complained to his brothers. "You just don't like to cook, and you think that I am going to end up doing it all. I don't like this business one bit."

"You just wait until your turn comes tomorrow," they both said. "Then you'll find out who's telling the truth."

Again they had a supper of cold leftovers and went on to bed for the night not too happy about what they had eaten.

Now, the next day, sure enough, it was Jack's turn to cook. As soon as Tom and Will had set out for the newground, he started to work. He was so hungry from the past two days that he was really going to do it up right today.

Jack went out and killed a chicken and cut it up to fry. He fixed some leather-britches beans and some creasy-greens. He made a great big pan of cornbread to go with it all. When the cornbread was just nearly right, he went out the door and started hammering on that railroad rail bell.

Jack stood there and looked down the road for his brothers. Instead of Tom and Will, he saw coming right up there toward the house this great big old giant with that long blue beard. He was headed right toward Jack like he was going to eat both the food and Jack in just about one big bite.

He did look scary, but Jack did not run to hide. Instead he looked at the big old man and hollered, "Hey, Uncle … how about coming on in the house to have dinner with us. We've got plenty to go around!"

With that, the big old man stopped right in his tracks. He looked at Jack; then he turned around and took off out of there like he was scared to death of who knows what.

This got Jack so bold that he decided to follow that man and find out who he was and where he was coming from.

The big old blue-bearded man was so huge and heavy that he couldn't move very fast as he walked, so Jack had no trouble following him as he went down the road and then disappeared into the woods. Jack trailed him through the woods until he saw the huge man disappear right out of sight into the ground.

When Jack got up to where the man had disappeared, he found that there was a big hole in the ground that he had never seen before. In fact, he had never even been in this part of the woods before.

Jack went up to the hole and looked down into it. It was just dark, and he couldn't see where it went. He picked up some rocks, dropped them into the hole, and never even heard them hit the bottom. They just sounded like they fell forever. "Tom and Will have got to see this," he thought to himself as he started back home.

In the meantime, Tom and Will themselves had gotten back to the house and couldn't find Jack. He had taken off in such a hurry that he left the door standing open, and, of course, all the food was still on the stove. The only thing that Tom and Will could think was that maybe that big old blue-bearded man had come and, this time, had eat up Jack instead of the dinner food. The two of them were just sitting there and crying about their lost brother when Jack came walking back in the door.

"Where have you been?" Tom said. "We thought you were all eat up!"

"Let me tell you," Jack started. "Both of you were telling the truth for sure. I am just sorry that I didn't believe you about that old man."

"He came again, did he? How did you get rid of him?"

Jack told them exactly what had happened. Then he said, "I want to go down in that hole and find out where he went. Come on, let's get some stuff together and I'll show you where he went."

After they gathered together a big wooden bucket and all the long pieces of rope they could find, the three started off down the road and through the woods with old Jack in the lead. He took them right straight up to that hole in the woods where the bearded man had disappeared. Jack dropped a few rocks down the hole to show Tom and Will how deep it was. Then he told them his plan.

"I want you two to stay up here and let me down in this hole until I hit the bottom," Jack told them as he tied the wooden bucket onto the end of the rope. He dropped the first few feet of the rope into the hole, then stood in the bucket and held onto the rope. "Now, just let me down real slow," he told Tom and Will. "I'll pull on the rope when I want you to pull me back up."

Jack's brothers let the rope out slowly until the first long length of it was all let out. In all that time Jack was still just dropping down through the dark without being able to see anything.

Tom tied on another length of rope and continued to let Jack on down into the hole.

About the time the second coil of rope ran out and the third length was tied on, Jack came out through a hole and saw that he was hanging down out of the sky of a whole new world down under the ground. He could see houses and farms and land all around there. When he looked back up to where he had come from, he could just see his rope disappearing up into the clouds.

It seemed to be light down there, but Jack couldn't see any sun or anything like that. He didn't know where the light was coming from.

Anyway, Tom and Will kept on letting the rope down until pretty soon Jack's bucket bumped right on the ground and he stepped out of it right in the side yard of what looked like a middle-sized farmhouse.

Jack walked up to the door of the house and knocked on it. He was going to ask a few questions and try to find out where he was.

When the door opened, Jack saw standing there the most beautiful girl he had ever seen in his life. She was just about his age, and when he saw her it was all he could do to keep from fainting dead away on the floor. Jack fell in love with her right on the spot.

After they talked a little bit and Jack had found out a few things about where he was, he learned that she was a serving girl in this house, and she was trying to work up to where she could go out on her own and seek her own fortune. Jack got an idea.

"Why don't you and I just go back up to the world on top and get married?"

"I would be glad to do that, Jack," she said. "There is just one thing.

"There is a huge old awful blue-bearded giant who lives down here, and I have a sister working in the next house down the road. It will go awful hard on her if I disappear out of here with you. I'll go, but you will have to get my sister out of here, too, or I can't stand to think about what might happen to her."

So Jack put this girl into the bucket and pulled on the rope. Tom and Will thought it was Jack wanting to come back up, so they pulled her up out of sight while Jack started down the road toward the next house to save her sister.

When this girl came out on the top of the ground, Tom and Will both fell in love with her at the same time. They would have had a fight over her right on the spot except that they remembered that Jack was still down there, and so they dropped the bucket back down the hole and waited for him to pull on it to come on up.

In the meanwhile, Jack got down the road to the house where the sister was supposed to be. He knocked on the door.

This door opened, and Jack had to hold onto the wall for a few minutes until he could start breathing again. There in the doorway stood a girl who had to be twice as beautiful as the first sister that he had found to begin with.

Jack forgot all about the first sister, and he was as in love with this one as he had ever even imagined he could be in his life.

He said to her, "Why don't you come on out of here and go back up to the world on top, and we can just get married and make our fortune together."

"That will be just fine," she smiled and answered Jack. "There is just one thing. I have a little sister who is working as a serving girl on the next farm. Where she works there is a great big old mean man with a long blue beard. He is the one that she works for.

"If I run off and get out of here, things will be awful hard on her. I would like to go with you, Jack, but I just can't leave knowing that my sister will be down here all by herself."

"Don't you worry about that," Jack told her. "The way we have to get out of here we can just go one at a time anyway. While you are going on up to the top to wait for me, I will just go down there and get your sister and send her on up out of here too."

So Jack took this new girl that he was now in love with and put her in the wooden bucket that had dropped back down through the hole. He pulled on the rope a few times, and Tom and Will took that as a signal and pulled her right up through the clouds and out of sight from where Jack stood watching.

Jack beat it down the road, looking for the farmhouse where the third sister lived. He was scared now because he knew that this was the actual house of the old blue-bearded man he had followed to start with, and he was not afraid for himself as much as that he might have trouble getting this last girl loose from the old man.

Finally he came to a big old house in the woods. He didn't go right up to the front door but instead went around to the kitchen door where the serving girl was more likely to be. Jack knocked on the door and then waited while he heard someone coming on the inside to open it.

Jack was not ready for what happened when that door opened. There in the door stood a girl that was at least three times as pretty as both the first girl and her sister put together. He lost his breath and went blind and passed out and fainted cold away on the floor and didn't come to until she splashed some cold water on his face with a dipper.

Even before he came to, Jack knew that he was in pretty bad love. When he could see that girl again, he knew for sure that this was the girl he was going to marry.

By now he had forgotten all about her sisters. All that he knew was that he had to get her out of the old blue-bearded man's house so he could take her home and marry her.

Once Jack could keep his breath well enough to talk, he and this girl talked things over a little, and she did in fact agree that she would marry Jack if he could get her slipped out of the house and away from here before the old blue-bearded man woke up. She told Jack that he was asleep in the living room and that he was likely to wake up before suppertime, so they didn't have long to mess around getting out of here.

She and Jack slipped right out the back door and around the side of the house and went back up to where the bucket was hanging back down out of the sky on the long rope that went back up to where Tom and Will were.

Now, what Jack didn't know was that up on top Tom and Will had completely fallen both in love with the second sister.

They were fighting over her like everything, and she liked it so much that she herself didn't care if Jack showed up later or not.

While Jack and the third girl were going up to where the traveling bucket was, she pulled a piece of red ribbon out of her pocket and braided it in her hair. "Jack," she said, "when you get back up to the top, you can remember which one I am by this red ribbon in case you are to forget for some reason. I'll not take it out of my hair until we can get married."

Then, just before she got in the bucket, she reached in her pocket and pulled out a gold ring. She handed it to Jack and said, "Jack, this is a wishing ring. You wear this and turn it around your finger when you get to wishing. If you are really wishing for something good for somebody besides yourself, it will help it to happen. It always helps for you not to just think about yourself, Jack."

Jack didn't have any idea that the wishing ring would work, but it would remind him of this girl until he could get back up to the top and get married to her. He slipped it on his finger and then helped her to get settled in the bucket. Then he pulled on the rope, and up she went out of sight.

Jack stood there and waited. He figured that in just a few minutes the bucket would come falling back down out of the sky and he would be out of there.

What he didn't know was that when this third girl got to the top of the hole, Tom and Will fell so much in love with her that they forgot all about the first girls and started fighting over her. Besides that, they were so busy fighting over this new girl that they completely didn't even think about dropping the bucket back down the hole so that Jack could get pulled up out of there.

He waited and waited for the rest of the day. When it got dark that night, he knew that even if the rope dropped back he couldn't see it. So he went inside the house that was right there and found him something to eat. Then he hunted up a bed and crawled right in and went sound to sleep.

Jack heard a big noise that waked him up from his sleeping, and he just had time to sit up in bed when the door to the room flew open. There, with a light-wood torch in his hand, stood the big old ugly blue-bearded man.

"Aaahhh!" he said, pointing the burning torch at Jack. "I thought I smelled a little old clean boy! Nothing in this land smells as bad as a clean boy ... unless it's the smell of a clean girl!

"Get out of that bed. I'm going to wait a few days until you are real good and dirty, and then I am going to cook you and eat you right up."

The old blue-bearded man grabbed Jack up under one arm and carried him off through the woods to the house where that third sister had come from. Once there, he locked Jack up in the chicken house where he was going to have to stay until he was dirty enough to satisfy the old man that he was fit to cook and eat.

Poor old Jack just didn't know what he was going to do.

Back up on the top of the earth, Tom and Will had finally stopped fighting over those girls. They had kind of paired up with the first two and let the third one alone because all that she could talk about was old Jack. They had finally let the rope and the bucket back down the hole, but this didn't do any good at all with Jack locked up on the old man's chicken house.

So Jack sat there in the chicken coop, day after day. The only person he ever saw was the old blue-bearded man when that ugly fellow came every day to bring him some food and smell to see if he thought Jack was dirty enough to eat yet.

One day Jack was getting so skinny that he noticed his gold ring sort of rattling on his finger. He turned the ring a few times, then remembered where he had got it and all the business about its being a wishing ring.

"Wishing ring, hah!" he said to himself. "If this is a wishing ring, I wish I was out of here!" Of course nothing at all happened because Jack was wishing for something for himself.

Later on that day Jack got to missing his brothers. " I wish that my brothers knew I was here," he said. And at that very moment Tom and Will and the three sisters were talking about where Jack might be and how they would all be happy if he could get back home and they could all marry the girl that was right for each one of them.

After a while Jack remembered about those two first sisters. He said to himself, "Those first two girls would be good for my brothers Tom and Will. I wish they could get married to Tom and Will." Jack had no way of knowing that on the very next day Tom and Will did indeed go ahead and marry the first two sisters.

He still sat there, locked up, day after day. Up on top of the world, the youngest of the sisters still had the red ribbon braided into her hair. She thought about Jack every day and thought that if he could just come back so they could get married, she would be the happiest person in the world.

One day old Jack was feeling mighty sorry for himself. He was sitting in the chicken house, getting skinnier all the time and smelling worse and worse.

As he sat there turning that ring around his finger and talking out loud to himself, he said, "I do so remember that girl with the red ribbon in her hair. Wherever she finally got to, I wish she could get to have whatever she wants to make her the happiest girl in the world."

At that very moment Jack was standing right back at home. There he saw Tom and Will, with the first two sisters as their wives. And there he saw that last beautiful sister with the red ribbon in her hair, still waiting to marry him.

He had finally wished on the ring for something for someone else, and it turned out to be the very thing that brought him home and saved his life.

Jack and that girl got married. All six of them lived right on there for a good long while. And they never did see that old blue-bearded man again. In fact, the hole seemed to have just disappeared in the woods where Jack had gone down to start with, and sometimes it is hard for Jack even to get people to believe the story of where his wife came from.

The Time Jack Solved the Hardest Riddle

Another of those times when I finally realized that I knew some stories not generally heard by all children came upon reading the "Wife of Bath's Tale." And later, when I heard the story of Lady Ragnell, I again recalled an old story about Jack. Here is that tale, one in which fortune is not as important as usual and several identity questions seem to take the front seat.

O ne time, when Jack was a fairly grown-up man, he was off walking through the world looking for his fortune. He had by now been around quite a bit and had seen an awful lot of things. But he still was looking out for things he had not even thought about seeing so far.

On this particular day, Jack was walking along through an old, thick forest, just looking to see where the road he was on might lead. It was all peaceful and quiet except for a few birds singing and a little warm wind blowing.

Jack sure was enjoying this nice spring day and was really not caring where this road might take him. Anywhere in the world would be a fine place to be on a fine day like this.

As he wandered along, Jack was enjoying the smells and sights and sounds, when all of a sudden he heard a sound he couldn't quite figure out. It sounded like some kind of a high and worn-out crying. Jack stopped right where he was and listened. He heard it again.

"Heeeelp!... heeeelp!" was what the sound seemed like to Jack.

Jack tried to figure out where the crying was coming from. Since it got louder as he walked along, he kept going toward where he could hear it stronger.

In just a few steps Jack came out in the clearing of an old house-site. The house was gone except for what was left of the chimney stones, and the vines and undergrowth had covered over most other signs that anybody had ever lived there.

"Heeelp!" the cry came to him again. It sounded like it was coming from behind the old chimney of the fallen-down house. Jack walked around there, and then he saw the top of an old well. All the weeds were stomped down around the old well like there had recently been some people doing something around there. When Jack got up to the well, he saw that there was a flat lid over the top of the hole, with a great big rock on top of that lid. Whoever was doing that crying was down in that well for sure.

Jack wasn't real sure what he wanted to do about this, but he just couldn't walk away from here without doing something. So he pushed the big rock off of the top of the covered well and then lifted the lid off of the opening.

Now the cry really got louder. "Heelp!" it came as the sunlight poured down the open well. Jack looked down in there, and it was so deep and dark that he couldn't see one thing in the world.

He looked around for something to make a light out of. There was an old bucket on a rope by the top of the well, and Jack picked it up. He walked around there and picked up pine cones until he had filled the bucket up to the top with them.

Jack struck a light to the pine cones and then let the burning bucket down into the well so he could see what was down there.

By the light of that torch-bucket Jack could see that the well was dry. Then he saw there—at the bottom of the dry well—a young girl all tied up, with a gag worked just far enough off of her mouth so that she could holler.

Jack pulled the fire-bucket back up and took the rope loose from it. Then he tied one end of the rope to a tree and dropped the other end down that well. Now he climbed down that well, just going on memory about how far it was to the bottom.

In no time at all Jack had untied that girl, climbed back up the rope himself, then dropped it back to the bottom and pulled her up.

Once she was out in the sunlight, Jack saw that she wasn't just any girl. She was absolutely the most beautiful girl he had ever even thought about seeing in his entire life. He almost passed out, but instead, he just fell right in love with her right there on the spot.

"Who are you?" he asked her, when he could get his breath. "And how did you get down in that well?"

"Oh," she cried, "my name just doesn't matter anymore. I might as well not have a name by now. My father is dead and just buried in his grave yesterday, and already today my stepmother has had me tied up and thrown down in that well to die. Even if you got me out of there, I'm just too scared to go back to the castle."

Now, Jack had heard in the last town he had passed through that the king of that land had just died, and when he heard this, he knew that he had just met the dead king's daughter. It sounded like it didn't matter much who she was, though, with her stepmother trying to get rid of her like that.

"Well," Jack said, "then don't go back there."

"How will I live?" she cried.

"Come with me. I'm going along to seek my fortune, and you can do the same thing. We'll just try to come up with enough to eat and a few places to sleep, and we can see a lot of the world.

"You just never can tell what we might run into that could set us up for the rest of our lives."

The king's daughter wasn't too sure about this, but when she thought about what would happen if she went back to the castle, she decided that Jack had the best idea. There was just one problem.

"I'll go, Jack," she said, "but I don't have any clothes except what I have on my back. That might be well and good for you, but I can't get along with just one pair of shoes."

"That's no problem," said Jack, smiling at her. "We'll just sneak back up there to that castle in the dark tonight. Then we can slip in there, and you can get whatever you need out of your own stuff. Then we'll get out of there and never show up around here again."

It sounded like a good plan to both of them, so they decided that it was exactly the thing to do.

Jack shared what little food he had with the king's daughter, and they waited around that old house place until dark. Then, with her showing him the way, the two of them slipped up to where the castle was.

Now, this castle was up in the high land of the mountains, and there wasn't any moat around it. All the doors were closed up for the night, but the king's daughter knew which low windows were likely to be open. She and Jack found one in no time, and the two of them climbed right inside.

They ended up in the kitchen. This window was almost always left open to let in fresh air and so the fire would draw better.

Since she knew the way, it was easy to slip through the castle and up to the girl's old room. Lucky for her, the old stepqueen hadn't thrown her clothes out or even cleaned the room up yet. As sorry as that old woman was, she probably wouldn't ever get around to cleaning it out unless she could get something for what was in it.

The king's daughter had Jack help her, and she got an old traveling bag and packed it up with good, sturdy clothes that would hold up for walking and sleeping outdoors a lot. She also put a few other things like combs and hairbrushes and scissors and a mirror in the bag. Then she and Jack took off.

What they didn't know was that the old stepqueen had watchmen keeping an eye on that old well, so she knew everything that had happened all afternoon. She was just watching and waiting for the time to catch them.

Jack and the king's daughter got through the kitchen and went to the very window they had crawled in to begin with. When they climbed back out, there was the old stepqueen right outside the window, waiting to catch them just as they were sure they were all safe.

"Caught you!" she croaked. Grabbing the king's daughter, she said, "I've got you this time, you little scoundrel! You thought you could get away, eh? Well, I'll do away with you and for good this time!"

She handed the king's daughter over to two nasty-looking guards, and Jack just stood there like he was frozen in place while he watched them drag her off out of sight.

As she disappeared, Jack could hear her crying to him, "Jack, Jack ... with all the power of my true mother's heart, I shall not die while we're apart." Then she was gone.

Jack stood there, held by two other ugly guards. There was nothing he could do.

Then the evil stepqueen spoke. "You, Jack ... you shall not die. I shall keep you for a while to use as my plaything. It would be a waste of a fine plaything to just kill you along with that stepdaughter of mine. I have waited long enough to get rid of her.

Then Jack was thrown into a dungeon. He had no way of having any idea what might happen to him next, and he had no idea what was happening to the king's daughter or where she might be if he could get out to try to help her.

The next day Jack was taken out of the dungeon and led up to see the stepqueen.

"What did you do with the king's daughter?" he hollered at her. "You better let her loose right now or you will be sorry." Jack couldn't believe that he was talking like this to somebody who would surely just as soon kill him as spit.

"Don't you worry, Jack. I haven't had her killed, yet! I decided to keep her alive because that would be more fun than anything with what I've got planned." Jack couldn't figure out what she was talking about.

"This," the stepqueen started explaining to Jack, "this is what I am going to do.

"Jack, you have the choice to keep the king's daughter alive. You may decide to die if you want to, and then I will just kill both of you. *Or,* you can marry *me,* and I will keep the king's daughter alive. Marry me and she will get to live right here in the castle with the two of us ... but you can't touch her!"

At first Jack thought that it would be better to just die. But then he realized that that might be all right for him; but if he decided to die, the king's daughter would die, too. That wouldn't be fair.

"How about giving me a little time to think about it," Jack said.

"Sure, Jack," the stepqueen said. "You can have until tomorrow. Then you will have to make up your mind. Marry me or die."

Jack was put back in the dungeon. Late that night he heard someone crying, and he realized that the king's daughter was locked up somewhere close by. He called out to her, and the two of them discovered that they were just on opposite sides of the wall from one another.

Jack got her to stop crying, and then he told her what the old stepqueen had planned. She started to cry again, but Jack told her to stop and to tell him everything she could about the stepqueen so that maybe he could figure out some way to deal with her in the morning.

"Tell me the things she likes more than anything in the world," Jack asked the king's daughter. "That way maybe I can come up with something to use on her."

The king's daughter thought and thought. Then she said to Jack, "A riddle, Jack. A riddle. My stepmother cannot resist a riddle. I think if you could ask her some riddles that she couldn't get the answer to, she just wouldn't be able to kill you until she could find out."

Jack stayed awake all night working on his plan. By morning he had about put it together. Maybe it wouldn't work, but at least Jack knew he was going to try.

About the middle of the next morning, Jack was taken down to see the stepqueen. Before she had a chance to say anything to him, he was talking to her. "Ma'am," Jack said very politely, "I was just wondering, a woman as smart as you are, do you like riddles?"

"Riddles?" she asked. "Did you say riddles? Why, Jack, I know every riddle in the world. You couldn't come up with a riddle that I couldn't solve!"

"If that is true," Jack half smiled, "then you wouldn't mind having a riddle contest with me."

"Of course I'd like a riddle contest. Just tell me what your deal is about riddles, and I will take you on for anything. You can't keep up with me with riddles," the stepqueen bragged.

This was exactly what Jack was hoping for.

"Let's have a riddle contest," he said. "If you win, I will marry you the way you want me to. But if I win, you shall let me go and the king's daughter can go with me. We will get out of here and you'll never see us again."

"That's a pretty good deal, Jack," she said. "You just don't have a chance, though. That can be our contest. Three riddles apiece to see who wins. And Jack, you get to ask me a riddle first."

Jack thought and thought. Then he started his first riddle. "You throw away the outside and cook the inside; then you eat the outside and throw away the inside. What is it?"

The old stepqueen hardly thought for a moment. "Why, it's an ear of corn, of course. Throw away the shucks and boil the ear, then eat the corn and throw away the cob! Pretty good, Jack. My turn!

"Fat as a dog-tick but thin as can be, round like the letter O but shaped like a C. What is it?"

"That's the moon," Jack said. "That was easy. Waxing and waning from fat to thin, sometimes full and sometimes a thin crescent. Now, it's my turn again." This was almost getting to be fun.

Jack spoke up for his second riddle. "Twenty white horses upon a red hill, themselves they eat nothing but others they fill. What is it?"

"What is it? What is it?" the old stepqueen thought out loud. "I know I can get it."

Jack was almost afraid to smile. Then the old stepqueen cackled, "I know ... *teeth!* Twenty chomping teeth on red gums. They don't eat anything themselves, but they sure do work to fill up the people who have them."

Jack was getting right discouraged by now. He was about out of riddles and answers, too. This old one was awful tricky.

"Now, I have one for you," the old stepqueen went on.

"What has never been seen or heard or felt or smelled or tasted by anyone, yet has filled everyone with fear?"

Jack was stumped. What could there even be in the world that you couldn't see or hear or feel or smell or taste? Especially something that could fill people with fear.

Then he remembered his awful night in the dungeon of the castle. It was a night that was made more horrible by the darkness that was so thick and heavy that it made it almost hard to move.

"I know!" Jack almost shouted, "it's *the dark!* No one can see or hear or smell or taste or feel the dark, but sometime or another it sure has scared everybody."

There was only one riddle each to go. Jack had just one more chance to fool the stepqueen. He had saved his hardest riddle for now. Surely the old woman wouldn't know the answer to this one.

Jack was ready. "What," he started the last question, "what do men desire above all else?" he asked the stepqueen.

"That old riddle?" she laughed. "You want to know the answer to that? Why, I thought you would have asked that silly riddle first! Everybody knows that. What do men desire above all else? Why, they desire women who will love them exactly as they love themselves!"

So she did know! Jack was brokenhearted. He was all out of riddles, and she still had one more to go. She was getting ready to ask it now.

"What," she asked Jack, "if a woman should desire to spend all of her life with one man, what, above all else, would she desire about that man?"

Jack thought and thought. He had never even thought about a question like this. Finally he tried out an answer. "How about this?" he said to the stepqueen. "What the woman would desire is that this one man love her exactly as she loves herself?"

"No, silly boy. Women are smarter than that. No woman wants to be loved as she loves herself. Women want better than that. Try again!"

Jack did try to answer the riddle again and again. He guessed everything he could think of, from providing wealth to health to happiness, but none of his answers was right.

Finally the old stepqueen said to him, "It sure is fine to see you suffer, Jack. This is so much fun that I'd like to draw this game out for a while. I'll make a deal with you. I'm not going to kill you because you can't figure the riddle out right now, Jack. I'm going to give you a year to suffer!

"Yes, Jack, I will keep the king's daughter locked up for one year while you go all over the world trying to find out the answer to my last riddle. If you can come back with the right answer, then I will let you both loose. But if you can't find out in a year, then you will have to marry me right on the spot.

"I am sure going to enjoy this year, Jack."

So Jack was sent on his way to wander and search the world for a year, trying to find out what women would desire above all else if they should want to spend their life with one man.

As soon as Jack was out of sight, the stepqueen sent for the king's girl. "Well," she said to the daughter, "your true love, old Jack, is gone off and left you. He'll not be back again, so it's time to get rid of you for good!"

The stepqueen had the king's daughter taken back to the same dry well where Jack had found her. This time she was chained down in the bottom of the well and gagged so tight that she couldn't possibly make a sound. Also, this time, instead of the cover of the well's being weighted by one rock, a whole pile of heavy rocks was piled to cover the well so completely that you couldn't even tell that the well had ever been there.

The king's daughter just cried and cried, not as much because of what had happened to her as because she just couldn't believe that Jack was gone. She didn't have any way to know why he was gone or what he had been sent out to do.

Back at the castle, the stepqueen knew for sure that the king's daughter wouldn't be alive for long. She didn't know that the king's daughter could not die. This was because her real mother, on her death bed, had given the girl a promise that in death she would try to grant her one wish. And the stepqueen didn't know that one wish had been made when the daughter promised Jack she would never die while they were apart. Nothing could kill her now until Jack came back to her.

Jack wandered around most of that part of the world. He walked on from town to town and from one village to the next. Even from one country to another he went trying to find somebody who knew the right answer to the riddle, "If a woman should want to spend her life with just one man, what would she desire in that man above all else?"

Of course, everybody he met had an answer for him. But all of these answers just seemed like they got Jack more confused instead of helping him any.

People said things like "giving her everlasting beauty" and "making her the queen of a big country." They told him everything from providing wealth to health to children. But none of these answers really sounded to Jack like they would satisfy the riddle.

It seemed to Jack like this year went by awful fast. It was almost over, and still he didn't have any idea what the answer to the riddle was.

Finally the day was coming when Jack had to start back to the stepqueen's castle. He thought that the king's daughter was still being held there just waiting for him to get back and that if he didn't get back on time the stepqueen would kill her. He didn't know that the stepqueen had already tried and actually thought that she had killed the one Jack spent every day thinking about.

Jack started his travels back toward the stepqueen's castle, still not knowing what the answer to the riddle was. He walked on and on for days.

By chance, Jack happened to be headed back toward the castle along the very same road that he had taken when he first came into this country over a year ago. In fact, the path he was taking was the same one that had taken him past that old house-site where he had first discovered the king's daughter in that dry well to begin with.

When Jack realized where he was, his heart almost gave out on him. He had tears in his eyes as he walked past the old fallen chimney and around it just to remember again where this stuff had all started.

A lot of the rocks that the stepqueen's men had piled up over the old well had fallen down through the year, but still Jack could hardly tell where the opening to the well had been. Jack just stood there and started crying as he thought about all the things that had happened since he had been here last.

While Jack was crying, he thought he heard an echo. Then he realized that he was actually hearing a crying sound made by something or somebody else. When Jack listened carefully, it sounded to him like the crying was coming up from inside the well.

Jack started moving the rocks off the cover of the well. He didn't know what was going on down there, but when he remembered what had happened to the king's daughter before, he sure wasn't going to leave here with that sound coming out of there. He didn't have any way of even guessing what he might find.

After Jack got all the rocks moved, he pulled the cover back off of the well. Then he tied a rope he had to a tree and climbed down inside.

All Jack found when he got to the bottom was a pile of human bones, some of them chained to the wall. They were as dry and as dead as could be. Nobody was down there.

Then Jack heard the sighing sound again. He listened and looked, and it seemed to be coming from the mouth of the dry skull. The voice said, "Gather my bones and lay me out ..."

Jack quickly gathered all of the bones he could see together and put them in the best order that he could. He laid them out on the ground from the skull to the toe bone and as he placed them in the right order they joined themselves together into a whole moving skeleton.

Then the skeleton spoke to Jack. "Give me something to drink ... something to eat ..."

Jack brought water to the skeleton and poured it into the mouth of the skull. Then he took some food from his bag and placed the food in the skull's mouth. As he fed the skeleton, it began to take on flesh and skin until, in just a few moments, there appeared before him the form of a shriveled old woman.

The wrinkled, old-looking woman spoke to Jack. "Thank you. You have helped me, and now I must help you.

"I do not have great magic power, but the power that is mine is also yours. What can I do to repay you?"

Jack thought for a few moments. He did not understand any of this. Then he remembered the riddle he had spent the year trying to solve.

"The only thing in the world that I need right now," Jack said, "is the answer to a riddle. If you can help me get the answer to that riddle, you will be making the difference for me between life and worse than death."

"Let me hear it," the ugly woman said.

"This is it," Jack said. "If a woman should want to spend her life with only one man, what should she desire in that man?"

The old-looking woman repeated. "That is a hard one.

"I cannot tell you what *all* women would desire. I do not know what all women desire. I can only tell you what I would desire above all else."

"What would that be? If it is different from all the things I have heard, then it would be worth a try."

The woman looked at Jack. "Above all else," she started slowly, "what I would desire is to have as my one lover a man whom I could truly call my friend."

Then the old woman seemed to disappear into the woods and was gone.

"Well," Jack thought, "that's not like any answer that I have ever heard before. I just don't know what to think about that."

He hurried on now back toward the stepqueen's castle as this was the last day of his year. He had collected a hundred answers to the riddle as he had traveled, but he was still not sure that he had learned the one that would rescue the king's daughter and save him from having to marry the stepqueen. He had to try, though.

Jack entered the castle, and the stepqueen met him on the spot. "Where is the king's daughter?" he asked.

"She will be here if and when the time comes," she answered. She thought that the king's daughter had been dead a long time by now. "Let's get on with the riddle!"

The stepqueen looked at Jack and said, "Well, have you found out? What is it that all women desire above all else? Take as many guesses as you like, Jack. You'll never get it."

And so Jack began to guess. "Wealth ... health ... beauty ... happiness?"

Every answer that he tried was wrong. "Keep guessing!" laughed the stepqueen.

Finally Jack had used up every answer that he had heard in all the world except the strange answer given to him by the ugly, old-looking woman who had come back to life in the dry well. So he looked at the stepqueen and started to speak again.

"Could it be," he said, "that if a woman should seek to spend her life with one man, that man could be called her lover but would have to be above all else called her *friend?*"

The old stepqueen never spoke a word. She, who had known many lovers but never a friend, was taken by a chill which froze all the boiling blood in her angry body, and she fell to the floor. When she did, her cold, stiff body shattered and the pieces scattered over the floor.

Instantly Jack started through the castle to search for the king's daughter. He didn't know what might happen next.

Before he could leave that very room, though, there appeared that same little wrinkled old-looking woman he had rescued from the well.

"Well, Jack," she spoke his name, "now you are free to search for the one whom you want to make your lover?"

"I'm looking for the king's daughter," he said.

"Of course," she said, "but before you go, Jack, look at me and tell me what you think of me."

Jack looked at her, and she was old and shriveled and horribly ugly in the light of day. Then he said, "I do not even have to look at you to tell what I think of you. For even when I only think of you, I know that you have been and are my *friend*."

With that, the old-looking woman changed, and the king's daughter whom he was looking for appeared right in front of him. Then he knew that he had given the right answer not once but twice.

Before that very day was over, Jack and the king's daughter were married. And from that day on they called one another both lover *and* friend.

The Time Jack Went Up
in the Big Tree

The following tale was always the most imaginative story about Jack I ever heard. As fascinating as it was to find a new world under the ground, it was even more impressive to find one up in the sky. It is a long story which sometimes was not finished in one telling. The graphic images it called into my head as a child are still there.

One time after Jack had grown all the way up and left home for good, he was on the road seeking his fortune again. He had held a pretty good job in a little town where he had worked for a while in a blacksmith's shop. It was not bad working there if all you wanted to work for was money, but Jack had this idea that he really wanted to get into something on his own and not be tied up to anybody else. Besides that, he needed to see some more of the world.

So Jack had the blacksmith bring his wages up to date, told that man goodbye, and started out.

Jack had bought a couple of loaves of bread and a big hunk of cheese with him to eat as he went on his way. He started out the first morning and walked all through the day. Working in that blacksmith shop had made Jack so tough that he covered quite a few miles walking on that first day alone.

Still he was tired out at the end of the day. He ate one of his loaves of bread and about half of that chunk of cheese. After washing his face in the creek, Jack found a soft layer of pine needles in a thicket. He spread his coat there on the ground and fell fast asleep.

About daylight the next morning, Jack woke up. He was ready to get on his way again. He walked about all this day and passed through two or three little towns. They just didn't look like the kinds of places where Jack thought he wanted to live, though, so he kept right on walking.

Late in the afternoon of this second day, Jack got to thinking about how he hadn't seen anybody or met anybody on the road for about that whole afternoon. Then, just about as soon as he thought about that, he came around a curve in the road, and right there in the middle he saw a little old bent-over woman trying to pick something up.

As Jack got closer he saw that she must have been carrying a big load of kindling wood sticks that she had picked up in the woods. The woman had dropped the whole load and was fighting hard to gather them all back up. She was bent-over in the back anyway and so stiff that it looked like she was having an awful time gathering up her load again.

About then she saw Jack. Before she even had time to say a word to him, he spoke to her. "You look like you need a little help, Ma'am. If you don't mind, I think I'll just pick up that load for you."

She thanked Jack, and with both his big hands he picked that load of wood up all at one time. "Which way are you going?" he asked her.

"Same way that you are," she said. Jack didn't stop to think that she didn't know where he was going since he didn't even know that for himself.

"In that case," he told her, "I'll just walk along with you and carry this wood. Where do you live?"

"Just a little piece down the road," she said. "Soon as we cross the river we'll be there.

Well, that old, bent woman and Jack walked on right slow, like just a-talking about everything under the sun. Jack didn't have any trouble at all carrying her wood and keeping up with her at the same time.

Pretty soon they started down a slope which Jack thought must lead to the river. It did. When they came to the river, it was a whole lot wider and bigger than Jack had imagined. Besides that, it had rained pretty hard the night before so that it was sure plumb full as it could be.

The old woman told Jack that it looked to her like the water was too high to cross. Before he even answered, Jack just picked her right up under one of his arms and carried her right across. Then he waded back and carried her kindling wood across.

Once they were both on the other side of the river, it was just a short walk on up to a little cabin where the old, bent woman lived.

"This is where I live, Jack. I'd be pleased if you'd come in and visit for a spell."

"Why, thank you," said Jack, taking her up on it. "I could use a little rest after walking all day today." She opened the door, and Jack carried that kindling wood right in the house. He broke it up into little pieces and piled it all in the woodbox beside the stove.

"Jack," she said, "you sure have been mighty good to me today. I sure would like to ask you to stay for supper, but I do not have one single thing in this house to eat. I haven't eaten all this day, and I guess that for my size I'm about as hungry as you are."

"Well," Jack said, "you are in luck. I have a little food with me that I can share with you."

So Jack got out his last half-a-loaf of bread and what little bit was left of that hunk of cheese. He put it on the table, carved it up, and the two of them shared the rest of that bread and cheese for their supper. Jack was plumb surprised at how full he felt after sharing just that little bit of food. He also thought that the little old bent woman looked a lot straighter and healthier than she had before she ate anything.

"You have been so nice, Jack," she said to him, "that I would like to offer you a place to spend the night."

Jack was feeling sleepy by now. "I sure would appreciate that," he answered her.

The old, bent woman took Jack out into a little lean-to room on the back of the house and showed him a narrow bed that was there. She told him goodnight, and then she said, "Jack, I do want to do something for you that will help you seek your fortune.

"When you wake up in the morning, just look around you and you'll figure out what it is." Then she went off to her bed, and Jack fell sound asleep.

Jack slept just about as well that night as he ever had slept in his life. He was surely rested through and through when he woke up in the next morning.

Just as soon as he was awake, before he even got his eyes open, Jack had a strange feeling about where he was. He could feel a breeze blowing across his face like he was sleeping in the out-of-doors. Besides this, he could hear birds singing and bees humming, and he could smell flowers. It did seem like he was sleeping right out in the woods.

Jack opened his eyes. It was no wonder that he had the strange feeling because he *was* right out in the woods.

The little log house was gone; the little old bent-over woman was gone; even the road he had walked on to get here was gone. He was sleeping on the moss right out in the wild middle of the woods.

Jack stood up and looked around. As far as he could see in every direction, there was nothing at all but thick, deep woods.

There was not a single sign of a trail or path or road in any direction. Jack couldn't tell which way he had come. He couldn't tell one way from another.

Then, as Jack looked behind where he had been sleeping, he saw it. What he saw was the biggest tree he had ever seen or imagined in his life. Jack hadn't noticed the tree at first because he had been asleep with his back to it. But now he saw it.

This big tree was at least as big around as a house, and it just went on and on and on out of sight up into the sky. It disappeared into the clouds before Jack could begin to tell how far up the top was.

Jack wondered out loud, "Is that what that little old bent woman was talking about when she said she would do something to help me out with my fortune?" Jack didn't know for sure, but there was one thing he did know. From the very time that he first saw it, Jack knew that he was going to try to climb it.

There were not any limbs on the big tree until it got way up past all the other trees in the woods, but the bark was so thick and had such big, wide cracks in it that Jack was sure he could climb the trunk using the bark for handholds and footholds. At least he sure could try.

And so Jack, right then and there, started up the tree.

"This is going to be easy!" he thought to himself. Even if this tree didn't have anything up in it, it was so tall that he could get up above the other trees around there and maybe see where he was.

Jack climbed up and up and up. The climbing really was easy. It was sometimes almost like somebody had made little steps for him to use on his way up. Jack went right up through the other trees until in no time he was all the way above all the rest of the forest.

It was such a clear day that Jack could see everywhere out over those treetops. He looked and looked, but no matter which direction he looked, he couldn't see anything that he recognized. There were just trees in every direction and mountains that he had never seen before. Nowhere was there any sign of a town or a farm or even a house all off by itself.

Then Jack looked up. He saw that he was just now beginning to climb this big tree. About halfway up to the cloud where the tree disappeared, Jack started coming to where some limbs were starting on the tree. This did make the climbing a lot easier.

Jack sure was glad that the wind wasn't blowing on this day, because he was so high up by now that he could see the earth curving away out of sight.

Once he got on up into the limbs, Jack didn't have any feeling of being up in the air anymore. Some of these limbs were so big that two people could have walked on them side by side without falling off.

Jack kept climbing until it was getting dark. When it was too dark to see anymore, he just settled down on a big, wide, moss-covered limb and went off to sleep right there. He wasn't scared at all about falling off. That limb was wider than any bed he had ever slept in. And the moss was so thick that it was a real good bed to sleep on.

Jack slept pretty well up in the big tree and woke up strong and rested in the light of the next morning. He sure was hungry, though. After thinking about how far he had come up to get to where he was, Jack thought that he might as well not go back down until he had climbed on up to see what was at the top. So he started climbing again, but now on an empty stomach.

As Jack climbed, the tree got even thicker. Limbs got bigger and bigger. He started seeing a lot of birds, and he could hear animals way off in the limbs.

About the middle of the day he started hearing voices right above him. Jack climbed on and came to two little men sitting on a limb and having some lunch.

"Well, who are you?" Jack asked.

"Who are *you?*" they asked right back.

"I am Jack. I've come up here to see where this tree goes. But right now I sure am hungry."

The little men gave Jack some of their food. After lunch they took him to the little town where they lived. It was built right there in that tree, except that they didn't call it a tree. All the people who lived in that tree called it "the world."

Now Jack was in a place where the big limbs were as wide as streets, with little houses built along on the sides.

Small sheep and cows grazed on the moss and ferns that grew on some of the wide limbs. They didn't need any fences up there. They just had gates where the limbs joined together.

There were pools of water that caught in the hollows and forks of the limbs. They were used for washing and cooking and for drinking. Some of the wide limbs were gardens, with corn and beans growing right in the deep moss. It was easy to string up the beans because they didn't need any stakes or posts.

Jack stayed there all day with those little people and spent the night with them. They told him that they had all been born right there in that little tree town. None of them had ever climbed very far down the tree in their lives because they had heard stories that if you went down too far you wouldn't be able to crawl back up.

A few of these little people had explored higher up, though. Some of their explorers who had gone up higher had never come back. Some of those who did come back told of a land of mystery and castles and magic and witches. A lot of the little people didn't believe this, but Jack had already decided that he was going to climb on higher and check this whole thing out.

After breakfast the next day, the little people packed up a sack of food for Jack and wished him good luck. He promised that he would try to come back and tell them what all he found on up there. Then he started out, climbing up to explore the higher lands of the big tree.

Jack climbed all day again. He stopped about noon and had a good dinner meal on the food the little people had packed up for him. Then he climbed on until it began to get dark. He started looking for a good, wide limb to sleep on. In a few minutes he found one. It was all covered and thick with moss. Jack settled down there, ate his supper, and in no time he was thinking about going to sleep for the night.

But before Jack got all the way to sleep, he heard a stirring noise. He looked toward where he heard the sound and thought he could see a light moving in the darkness way out on the wide limb he was sleeping on. This was a little bit strange to Jack, so he thought that he might as well try to see what it was before he went to sleep for the night.

It was real foggy by now—especially since Jack was way up in the clouds, being this far up in the tree—and he couldn't really see much in any direction. Jack felt his way out on the limb, and as he got closer he could see a little more clearly where the light seemed to be coming from. It was a big, square glow that looked an awful lot like it was coming from a window pane.

As Jack got closer, sure enough it was a window with a light glowing inside. It was so dark and foggy that he couldn't see anything at all about what kind of building it was in, though. He couldn't tell if it was a house or what. All he could tell was that it was big, that it was sitting on something below the limb Jack was on, and that it was made out of stone. He saw that this tree limb he was walking on grew right up to the window so close that he could touch it.

There didn't seem to be anything to do but to climb right in that window to try to see where he was.

Jack eased over to the window pane and pushed up the sash. He stepped right into that window without having any idea what he might find in there or even where he was to begin with.

What Jack found when he got in there was a young woman. She was not as old as Jack, and she was sitting in a chair with her head in her hands, crying. Jack scraped his feet on the floor to make a little noise so he wouldn't startle her by being too close when she saw him. At the sound, the young woman looked up. She didn't seem to be scared or even surprised at all to see Jack there.

"Hello," she said. "I don't know who you are, but whoever you are, I am glad to see you!"

"I'm Jack," Jack told her. "Who are you? And where in the world are we?"

"I am the daughter of the king who used to own this country and run this place. This is my castle now, and I have lived here all of my life."

For the rest of that night Jack and that young woman talked. He told about his adventures, which she couldn't understand at all, since she thought that the limb outside the window was just the limb of a tree that grew up from an oak tree in the yard of this castle where they were now talking. Jack couldn't understand this either, but it seemed that he had somehow come out in a whole different world from where he had started.

The old king's daughter told Jack about how she lived as a prisoner in this very castle where they were now visiting.

It seemed that there was a bad king in the next country over who had wanted her to marry him. When she wouldn't do it, this bad king had killed both of her parents and now had her locked and bolted up in this castle twenty-four hours a day. She was afraid to try to go outside because there was a big pack of trained wolves that the bad king had living out in the forest to keep guard on the castle.

So she was, like she explained to Jack, under a curse to be in prison by herself in her own castle.

Now, the castle was kept supplied with food by the bad king. He didn't want her to die because he wanted to come and look at her once in a while. His servants kept her fed right well because the bad king figured that one of these days she would give up and marry him.

This was why she was so glad to see Jack. She didn't care who he was or where he was from. She was so lonesome for some company and somebody to talk with that she would have let anybody in. And besides that, there was enough food here for her to feed all the company that she would get.

Well, old Jack just stayed on there. The food was good, she gave him his own room, and they just talked and ate and visited and had a right good time for several days. After all, when Jack looked out the window in the morning after the first night, he saw that the limb he had come in on was indeed just an ordinary-looking limb on an oak tree, and he wouldn't have known how to get back to where he came from even if he wanted to.

One day, several days after his arrival, the king's daughter gave Jack a warning. "Jack," she started, "you may go into any part of this entire castle that you want to find out about. I know that you like to poke around and see what you can find. So you are free to wander and check all around everywhere you want to … except for one thing."

"And what is that?" Jack asked her.

"There is just one room that I have to ask you not to go into. It is the highest room at the very top of the stairs in the tallest tower on the back corner of the castle. Don't ever go in there!"

"Why not?" Jack asked her. "What is so different about that room? I'm not much afraid of anything, you know."

"Just don't ask," was all she answered. "Just don't you ever dare go in there. There is evil that can come out if you *ever* go in that room."

Now, by this time in his life Jack had had so many adventures that once he heard this he just couldn't wait until he got his first chance to look inside that one room.

It took him several days for that chance to come. That king's daughter liked having him there so much that she stayed right next to him just about every minute of the day and night.

About four days later, Jack got his chance. The king's daughter was taking a nap one afternoon, and, as soon as she was asleep, Jack headed right up those stairs for that highest tower.

He found the stairs that led there and started climbing. Up, up, up Jack went right toward the top of that highest tower in the castle.

Jack could tell that nobody had been there in a long time because the stairs were real heavy with dust, and cobwebs just went back and forth all over the place.

Finally he got to the top and to the door that he was told he should not ever even try to open.

It was all dark and quiet there. The dust was thick. Jack listened. He could not hear any sounds at all coming from beyond the door to show that anything or anybody was in there. Jack tried to look under the door and then through the keyhole. He couldn't see anything but darkness on the other side.

Jack took hold of the door latch and tried to turn it. It was locked! But then he looked up, and there he saw the edge of a key just sticking out over the ledge at the top of the door like somebody had tried to hide it up there.

He reached up and took hold of that key, and it fit right exactly into the keyhole in that door. When he turned the key, the lock turned over as easy as could be. Then Jack turned the latch-handle, and the door was free to swing open.

At first Jack could not see a thing inside the room. He stepped through the door and looked around him. It was fairly dark with the only light coming in through two small openings high up in the wall. Jack figured that this room must have once been used like a prison because he saw all kinds of chains fastened to the walls.

All of a sudden a strange sound made Jack's hair stand right up on end. "WWwww...rrrr!" it went. Jack spun around at the sound. "WWwwww...rrrrRRR!"

There, above Jack's head on the wall, was a large black bird. It was fastened to the wall by three of the iron rings that must have once been used to hold prisoners there. One of the rings was around the bird's neck, and the other two were around the creature's legs. The bird's huge black wings flapped free, but the bird couldn't go anywhere.

"WWhhh...rrrr!" it screeched at Jack. After he got over being startled the first time, Jack wasn't really scared anymore.

In fact, it sounded to him more like the big bird seemed sad and pleading.

"WWaaa...rrr!" the bird cried again. "Waa...rrr!"

"I just wonder what it's trying to say," Jack thought to himself.

"Waa...t...terrr! Wa...t...er!" the bird seemed to beg.

"Water!" Jack said out loud. "Of course! I should have known. What it wants is some water."

Jack seemed to have forgotten all about the warning that had been given to him by the king's daughter. He ran down and down the stairs to the kitchen, where he found a big dipper and a bucket of water. Back up the steps he went with the bucket and the dipper.

In the tower room once again, Jack dipped out some water and offered it to the begging black bird. The dry bird drank deeply and drained the dipper three times.

The water seemed to give the great black bird incredible strength. It flapped its wings, shrieked a horrible scream, then powerfully ripped all three of the binding iron rings off of the wall.

Once it was free, the bird flew straight for one of the window openings. It landed on the window sill and perched there for a moment while it turned to look at Jack. Then it spoke to him with a man's voice: "You have set me free. Now I shall have the king's daughter, whether she will have me or not!"

Then, in a split second, the black bird turned into a scowling and ugly man. He jumped out of the window and disappeared in a great crash of thunder, fire, and smoke which knocked Jack flat down on the floor. All at once the entire castle disappeared, and, with the castle gone out from under him, Jack was falling down and down and down toward the earth.

He hit the ground with a thud and turned to see a big clearing in the forest where the castle had once stood. Then he heard screams. He turned to see the ugly scowling man. He was carrying the king's daughter under one arm as he rode away on a big black horse that only had three legs.

This was all just about more than Jack could take in at one time. He just sat there on the ground for a while and tried to clear out his brain. He even pinched himself and slapped himself on the face to be sure he was awake and that this wasn't just some kind of dream. He thought out loud, "This is about more than my brain can take!"

After a little while Jack stood up. He was shaking all over still, but he could walk around all right in a few minutes. He didn't know where to start trying to figure out what had happened, how to find and rescue the king's daughter, or how to understand where he was and how he got there.

Finally he started off walking through the woods, going in the same direction that the three-legged horse had run in. The horse was pretty easy to track since, with just three legs—one in the front and two in the back—it made a funny set of tracks something like a big, hoofed rabbit.

Jack walked for a good while. Then he heard some moaning and groaning off in the woods. Jack went over toward the sound of the moaning to see what it was. There in the thicket of the woods beside a creek he found a big silver wolf with one of its front paws caught in a big steel trap. When the wolf saw Jack, it talked with the voice of an old man.

"Help me, help me, Jack!" said the wolf.

"How do you know my name?" Jack asked. "And besides, who are you, and *what* are you?"

"I know who you are because I watched you come here. Every day I have watched you come to fall in love with the old king's daughter. I live here in these woods, and I only look like I am a wolf. I can change from a wolf to a man, and I travel as a wolf so that I am safe from the evil king's wolves when I am traveling here in the forest. If you could help me get out of this trap, I will try to help you get on to where you want to go.

Jack thought that he might as well help the wolf out, so he got a big stick and pried the steel trap open.

As soon as the wolf was out, it licked its injured paw. Then it stood up on its hind legs and turned into a little old man. Jack was amazed.

"Help me figure out what's going on here," Jack begged the old man.

"Well," the old man shook his finger at Jack, "you have messed things up, Jack! You see, Jack, here in this world we all can change ourselves into different beings. But only when we are in normal shape can we change back. That's why I couldn't get to be a man again until you let me out of that steel trap.

"When you gave water to that thirsty bird ... that was a mistake, Jack.

"I know that the old king's daughter has probably told you about how she was trapped in the castle. Every day that evil, ugly king that wanted her to marry him would turn himself into some kind of awful animal and come to the castle where he would try to scare her into marrying him.

"One day he turned himself into that black vulture you saw trapped up there in the tower. On that day I turned myself into a mountain lion and caught him. Then the king's daughter and I locked him up in the castle tower. Being magic, he would not die, but he suffered enough from lack of food and water that he could not turn himself back into a man and get loose. That is, until you came along and helped him get loose, Jack.

"Now that he is loose and has carried off the king's daughter, I guess he's so mad about being locked up there that we won't ever see her again. He has already destroyed the whole castle, as you see.

"That three-legged horse is the fastest one in the countryside. While he's got it, you'll never catch him or have any chance of getting the king's daughter back."

"Then," Jack said, "you do mean that I have ruined everything. Is there anything at all that I can do to have even a hope of putting things back together again?"

"Well," the little man cocked his head, "let me think ... The only thing that I can come up with is for you to get a horse that is faster than the evil king's three-legged one. Maybe if you go where it came from, you can get another horse that is faster."

"Where is that?" Jack asked.

"It's a long way off, Jack, and dangerous besides that."

"I don't care how dangerous it is, or how far," Jack said. "I am the one who messed things up, so I want to go there and try to fix things. Now tell me where to go."

"Well," the old man said, "it is another land, way beyond here. It is a land that doesn't have a king but is ruled by a witch. She is a whole lot worse than even that king that now has the old king's daughter.

"Just go through these woods for three days until you come to a wide river, cross it, then follow the setting sun. In three more days after you cross the river, you will come to a little hut where she lives. She raises the fast horses, but she also has magic fighting pigs. They are what you have to watch out for. Those pigs are killers, Jack."

"Is that where the bad king's fast horse came from?" Jack asked.

"Yes it is," the old man answered. "That is part of the story. The bad king tricked that old witch out of her fastest horse. When he took off on that fast horse, she sent her own pack of wolves after him. They caught him just as he reached the river I was telling you about. They tore off one of the horse's legs, but since they can't cross the water, the king got away, and that's why the horse now has only three legs."

"Well, now," Jack said, "I think I've got a plan. If I can go there to where she lives and trade her out of a *four-legged* horse, I'll bet you it would be fast enough for me to catch him and get the king's daughter back. That's what I'm going to try, no matter how dangerous it is."

"Well, Jack," the old man said, "if you are going to go, then go prepared." The little old man turned to the steel trap where he was caught when he was a wolf. There were several silver wolf hairs stuck to the jaws of the steel trap. The old man plucked the wolf hairs from the steel jaws, counted out twelve, and handed them to Jack.

"Take these with you, Jack. Perhaps some of my magic will be able to help you."

"What do I do with these?" Jack asked.

"They will," the old man said, "they will stop danger which comes riding on the wind. There are three for the east wind, three for the west wind, three for the south wind, and three for the north wind. Care for them and they shall take care of you. Now, Jack, be on your way. Too much time has already passed."

With that, the little old man turned into a white bird and flew away, leaving Jack there alone with only the twelve silver wolf hairs to show him that he didn't just dream all of this up.

"Well," Jack said to himself, "I might as well get on my way over toward that river. I've got a long way to go and a lot to do if I am going to get that king's daughter back."

Off Jack went in the direction in which the little man had pointed. He traveled three days, and at last the wide river appeared, just as the little old man had promised. "This must be it," Jack answered himself.

Jack pulled off his boots and his socks, held them over his head, and waded in. The water wasn't very swift, and it never did get much over his waist. If he did manage to get a horse, he wouldn't have any trouble at all getting back across this river and onto this side again.

It was already late in the day, so it was easy to figure out the direction of the setting sun. So old Jack walked on that way for several hours until it finally did get really dark. He didn't see any bad wolves at all, but he did see three big reddish-looking pigs rooting under some oak trees for acorns.

Jack found a snug little cave to sleep in and slept pretty well. He was not too hungry because he had eaten a whole load of blackberries that he had come onto just before it got dark.

Early in the next morning he got up and got started walking away from the rising sun. He got a good bearing on a mountaintop so he could keep his direction straight all through the middle of the day as the sun drifted on overhead. Then in the afternoon he got his direction straight out by following the setting sun. Now he had one full day behind him, on top of the few hours he had walked in getting a head start the day before.

This night he slept under the trees in a big pine thicket. He slept fine because he hadn't seen any wolves at all, just three big white pigs rooting in the forest.

The next morning Jack started out again. He kept on eating a few nuts and berries, but he was beginning to get awful hungry. On to the west he walked until he had walked out all the daylight of this second full day. Tomorrow would be the third day, and since Jack had that first head start, he figured he would get to the witch's hut before the day was over.

Again this day Jack saw three pigs. These were sort of a bluish color. They were rooting along a low marshy creek like they were trying to keep cool. Still he didn't see any wolves, so he slept just fine on a bed of moss in a protected little hollow.

"Tomorrow," Jack thought, "I will finally get there. I sure do hope I can get something to eat from that witch. It won't do me any good to get a fast horse if I'm starved to death before I get it."

Jack started off eagerly the next morning. He was anxious to get on to find the home of that witch. After walking west for about three hours, Jack heard some pigs rooting in the trees. He walked over to where the noise was coming from and found three big black pigs. They weren't rooting but were eating some corn somebody had thrown out there for them.

Jack knew that he had to be close to the old witch's hut now. He started being right alert, on the lookout for anything strange from here on out.

In a few minutes he saw a trail leading along from where those pigs were. Then, up ahead, he saw smoke rising, like from a chimney. Jack walked on until he saw that witch's little hut.

It was in a pine thicket in a hollow, just a small hut made out of logs with a rock chimney at one end. It was a pretty high-peaked little house, like it probably had a sleeping loft inside above the main part.

There was a rail fence around the yard with just a stile to get over it. Behind the cabin there was a big hoglot just full of pigs and hogs of all sizes. The hoglot had an opening in the rails so the hogs could come in and out, or the hole could be stopped up with brush to make a gate.

Way over in the back was another big pen that was filled with horses. This pen was fastened to a big barn, and it sounded like there were more horses in the barn. The ones that he could see on the outside sure were beautiful and looked fast.

Jack sat down by a big rock so he could just study over this whole situation for a while before he figured out what to do next.

In a little while the door of that little hut opened. "Oh boy," Jack thought, "now I'm going to get to see the witch."

But instead of an old witch, out came a young girl not nearly as old as Jack. She was fairly ragged and dirty looking. But Jack thought that if she was cleaned up, she might look right nice. Jack figured that she might be either the witch's daughter or some kind of serving girl. Whoever she was, Jack thought that he might better try to get in good with her before he took on the old witch herself.

Well, that girl seemed to have a bucketful of corn, and she also seemed to be coming right on up that trail toward where Jack was. He just sat there on that rock and waited for her to come on up and find him.

The girl was sort of walking with her head down from the weight of that bucket of corn. So she didn't have her eyes up to where Jack was sitting on that rock. She got right on up to him almost without ever seeing that he was there.

"You need some help?" Jack said to the girl.

That girl dropped her bucket and nearly passed out at the same time. Jack had nearly scared her to death. "Who are you?" she said to Jack. "Where did you come from anyhow?"

"My name's Jack!" he said. "I'm wanting to get a good horse. I heard that you might have some here to sell or trade off."

Now, this girl kind of liked the looks of old Jack. He was the first person of any kind that she had seen in several years besides her old witch mama. She thought that she might help Jack out a little if she could.

The girl told Jack all about the setup there. Her mama was the witch of that whole land around. She told Jack that her mama would probably make him some kind of an offer to work out a horse. Then she said that Jack had better be on the lookout for tricks with her mama, no matter what the old woman promised.

Jack asked her if she didn't want to escape and get on out of here when he left. But she said she'd just stay. She wouldn't know how to get along anywhere else. After all, the old witch was her mama, and someday all this land would be hers after her mama was gone. But she said that she would try to help Jack because she had taken a liking to him.

"Now, Jack," she explained to him, "here's the plan. I'll go on back to the house and not say anything to mama about meeting or seeing you. She's in a pretty good mood today, so you come on up to the house in a little while and see if you can't make a horse deal with her.

"I'll try to let you know what to do after I hear what kind of deal she gives you." Then the old witch's girl headed on back to the house.

Jack stayed out there for about half an hour. Then he headed right on up there to the little house himself. Jack knocked right on the door, and in just a minute it opened. There stood the witch.

Once Jack got a look at her she didn't look very scary at all. She was just a little old stooped-over woman. Only one thing about her looked strange: her nose was long and sharp and turned up on the end just like a steel hook. It was all calloused and as hard-looking as a flint rock. "Better watch out for that nose!" Jack thought to himself.

"And who are you?" she croaked at Jack.

"I am Jack, and I am in need of a good horse. I've heard everywhere that you raise the finest horses in the whole country. I was wondering if we couldn't work out a deal for me to earn a horse by working for you." Jack could see that witch-daughter watching out at him from behind the kitchen stove.

"Well, Jack, that sounds good to me. I am always needing help of some kind or another. I believe we could make a deal.

"I'll tell you what. I have a big pen full of pigs out back that I'm raising for bacon. They've been bad to get out at night … or something has been stealing them off.

"Now, Jack, if you can spend three nights out there taking watch of my pigs, and if none of them get away or disappear, then I'll let you have your choice of any horse I've got. How about that?"

"That's fair enough," Jack said. "I'll start tonight."

The old witch invited Jack to come on in and eat. He sure was relieved because he was by now just about starved.

Jack could have outeaten any of that old witch's pigs, but he went kind of easy so the witch wouldn't be able to know how bad off he was.

After dinner the old witch went out to work with her horses, and Jack was left alone with the daughter. Jack was anxious to hear from her how she thought things were going and if she had any advice for him.

"I'll tell you, Jack," she said, "that old trick she's trying on you is one of her favorites. You have to stay awake all night or she'll find a way for some pigs to get out while you're asleep. Don't let her slip you any sleeping potion, and you'll make it all right. Just be sure that whatever you eat or drink is something you see us already eating and drinking, too."

Jack thought to himself, "It will be hard enough to stay up all night *without* a sleeping potion. This old woman is a tricky one, sure enough."

Well, evening came on and they all had a big supper. Jack was feeling a whole lot better now after having two meals in the same day. After supper the old witch took Jack out to the hoglot.

The fence around it was plenty stout. Nothing could possibly get through. The only way in or out either was through that hole in the fence that the old witch used for a pig gate. She kept it stopped up with brush to keep the pigs in and then pulled the limbs out to open it.

"Now, Jack," she said, "don't you let a single one of my pigs disappear or the whole deal's off."

"I'll do my best," Jack promised her. Then he set himself up a sort of camp right there by that brush-gate, built him a little fire to keep warm, and set in to wait out the night.

It was all quiet until a little after dark. Then Jack heard somebody's footsteps crunching along the dirt of the trail toward where he was. It was the old witch herself. She was carrying a clay jug with steam coming out of it.

"Hey there, Jack!" she said, "I thought you might be getting cold out here, so I brought some hot coffee to warm you up and keep you awake."

"I thank you for that, ma'am," Jack said to her. "You sure are looking out for me!" He took the jug and held it against him so he could feel as much of its warmth as he could.

After she wished him a good night, the old witch left. As soon as she was out of sight, Jack poured that coffee right into the slop-chute that emptied into the pig's food trough. Those pigs heard the sound and they came running. They thought they were getting some slop, so they walked over there and lapped up that coffee.

Sure enough, in five minutes every one of those pigs was sound asleep! That coffee had been sleepy coffee that the old witch had doctored up for Jack. When he saw that it was powerful enough to put every one of those pigs to sleep, it scared him just to think about what it could have done to him.

Now Jack laid down and acted like he was asleep to see what would happen next. In a minute or two, the old witch came slipping back up to where he was. She thought Jack was out cold from the sleepy coffee, so she pulled all of that brush out of the hole in the fence so that those pigs could run out if they wanted to. Then she left and went home.

Since the pigs were sound asleep but Jack was awake, he got right up and plugged the hole back up before any of them could get away. Now it was one night down and two to go to get the horse.

The next night, just after dark, the old witch showed up again. This time she had a big pot of stew for Jack.

"You missed your supper, Jack," she said. "I brought you what was left over." She handed the pot of stew to Jack.

It was so doped up that he just about fell asleep from the steam rising off of it.

As soon as the old witch left, Jack poured the stew in the slop-chute and put every one of those pigs sound to sleep.

Jack laid down and watched while the old witch pulled the brush out of the hole in the fence again. This time she dragged it way off into the woods. But, since the pigs were sound asleep, Jack had plenty of time to drag it back and stop up the hole before any pigs escaped.

Now that old witch was mad. She was mad enough after the first night, but after two in a row she was really mad. She hooted around all day and even rooted up the ground with her nose, but she didn't want Jack to see what a fit she was having since he had fooled her somehow. He stayed out of her way.

By suppertime Jack was getting awful hungry, so he went into the house and ate with the witch and her daughter. They talked a little about how this was Jack's last night to be tested and about how the third time was always the hardest of all. After supper Jack headed out to set up shop by the pigpen.

Sure enough, just about dark the old witch showed up. She was armed for business for certain this time. She had a pot of coffee, a pot of stew, *and* some big heavy quilts with her.

"You might as well be comfortable on your last night, Jack," she said. Then she gave him all of this stuff and wished him a good night.

Jack poured that coffee and that stew both right down the slop-chute. Then he curled up in those quilts to watch. He didn't know that the old witch had tricked him good this time. There wasn't a thing wrong with the coffee or the stew either one this time, and those pigs were as wide awake as ever. But ... those quilts were just full of sleepy powders, and in a minute Jack was out cold.

Pretty soon the old witch showed up. She pulled out the brush and hollered to the pigs, "Sooo—eeey! Sooo—eey! Pig-pigpig!!" Every one of those pigs of every size just ran right out of that hole and off into the woods.

Now, old Jack would have been done for if it hadn't been for one thing. That old witch's daughter had been watching all of this from the house.

While the witch was "soo-ey-ing" out at the pigpen, that girl took the rest of her mama's sleepy powders and just pow-dered her own mama's bed good with them. When the old witch got back in the bed, she went out cold just as soon as she lay down.

Then that witch's daughter ran back out there to the pigpen. She climbed in through that hole in the fence, then started hollering, "Pigpigpig, sooo—eeey, SOOoo—eee! pig!" With that, all of those pigs ran back out of the woods and straight back in the pen. Then she gathered up some brush and stopped the hole back up tight.

Jack slept right through all of it!

The next morning he woke up. He saw that the pigs were all safe and sound the way he thought they had been the whole night. Jack didn't ever even know about how that witch's daughter had saved the whole deal for him.

Finally the old witch slept off her sleepy-powder night. When she woke up she hopped right out of bed and headed out to where Jack was. She was expecting to find the hoglot empty and Jack crying about losing out on the deal to get a horse.

Instead, she found Jack stretched out and resting beside a little warmup fire he had built. The hole in the fence was all stopped up with brush, and all the pigs were inside the pen just a-squealing for slop.

The old witch started boiling! She couldn't figure out how Jack had done it. She started turning bright red she was so mad. She started blowing smoke out of her ears, and steam came out of her nose. She rooted up the ground all around the house with her hooked nose.

Now, while she was steaming and plowing the ground and pitching this old fit, the daughter came over to where Jack was.

"Hurry, Jack," she said, "before she runs out of steam and cools off. Run to the barn and get the horse that you want and take off out of here. If you want to be sure to get away, take the white mare with the black hourglass mark on her flank. She's the one mama always rides when she's in a hurry. That mare's got to be the fastest one that's out there. Now, go, Jack!"

Jack did thank her. Then while that witch was still rooting and snorting, he headed out for the horse barn.

As soon as he was in the barn, Jack found that white mare with the black hourglass on her flank and started looking around for a saddle. Right then at that moment, the witch's daughter came in toting a nice saddle all trimmed in silver and a nice bridle with a silver bit. She helped Jack saddle and bridle that horse right fast, and then he jumped on and took off for good.

The last thing Jack saw, besides that witch's daughter waving goodbye to him, was dirt just a-flying every which way as that old witch was snorting and nose-plowing right up a long hillside.

It didn't take long for Jack to realize that he had picked the right horse. This one could purely fly. She could jump creeks and tangles and thickets that were too wide or too thick to jump or run straight through.

Just about the time that Jack thought he was going to get clean away without running into any trouble, he felt a strong wind blow up from the east. It was so strong that he could barely stay on that mare. Then he saw trouble. Running with that wind, coming right straight towards him, were three big, sleek, black wolves! Jack didn't know what he was going to do.

Then he remembered that the little old man he had rescued from the steel trap had given him those magic wolf hairs to save him from danger that came on the winds.

Jack reached into his pocket and pulled out three of those wolf hairs and threw them into that east wind. In an instant that wind died down and those three wolves turned into three black pigs, grunting and rooting in the ground. They looked a suspicious lot like those same corn-fed pigs Jack had passed on the way in.

Jack rode on as fast as he could, trying to get out of there. Now the north wind started rising. Sure enough, in just a few minutes here came three blue wolves. They had ice on their fur like they had run right on the icy north wind all the way from the north pole.

Now Jack was ready. He tossed three more of the magic wolf-hairs into the north wind, and the wind dropped off. Instead of wolves, now there were three acorn-gobbling blue pigs.

"Now," Jack thought, "I'm onto the old witch's plan. Well, I've got six more magic wolf-hairs. That's enough to take care of all the pigs I saw on the way in."

Jack rode on. Sure enough, he was right. This time it was a warm south wind that was rising. That wind got hotter and hotter, and with it came three red wolves with eyes flashing and breath like fire.

Jack let loose of three more wolf hairs, right into the wind. Just as fast as he threw them, that wind died down—and instead of wolves there were three big red pigs just looking kind of dazed.

"Three more to go!" Jack thought. "It couldn't be much farther to the river from here."

Here came the west wind. And right on that wind came three wild-looking, solid-white wolves. They had big fangs and bristly hair like porcupine quills. These wolves were on the run after Jack. Jack pulled the last three of the magic wolf hairs out of his pocket and got ready to let them fly.

Then he got a shock. Only two wolf hairs were left. He must have dropped one somewhere along the way.

"Well," Jack thought, "I might as well get rid of two. I'd rather have to fight one than have to tangle with all three."

Jack threw the two wolf hairs. The wind died down to a breeze and two of those wolves turned into big, fat, white pigs. The wolf that was left took one look at those fat pigs and forgot all about Jack. He tore into them like he was going to a supper. Jack thought, "Of course. Any wolf would rather eat pork than horsemeat."

Jack looked ahead and there was the river. Three big splashing leaps and they were across!

Now ... on to find the evil king and somehow to rescue the good king's daughter.

Jack didn't know which way to go to get to where the bad king had taken that good king's daughter. The only thing he knew to do was to go back to where the castle had been and try to find some tracks or something to go on.

It didn't take long to get back there on this horse. She was surely the fastest thing that Jack had ever had hold of.

Jack got back to where the castle had disappeared and started looking for the three-legged horse tracks. He checked everywhere but couldn't find a sign that looked like what he was searching for.

Just as he was trying to figure out what to do next, a big white bird fluttered down and perched on a tree limb close by. The bird sang out a song, and Jack's horse walked right up and listened to that song like it meant something to her. The bird finished and then took off. There on the tree limb Jack saw what looked to him like a few loose silver wolf hairs.

Now this old horse lit out after that bird. The white bird wouldn't ever get too high or too far ahead to lead them. They followed it on for miles.

Then Jack began to notice funny tracks along on the ground. He looked closely and saw them to be, sure enough, three-legged horse tracks. Jack knew that he was going in the right direction.

In a while they came to the top of a little rise that looked out over a valley. Down in that valley Jack saw smoke rising from a chimney. "This must be the place," he thought to himself.

They started on down. Just then he heard a flapping, and out of the sky came diving a big black bird just like the one the old evil king had turned into when he flew out of that tower window to start with.

This black bird headed straight for that white bird that they had been following. It attacked the white bird and killed it there in mid-air. Jack watched as the white bird fell dead to the ground.

When that dead bird hit the ground, it turned in an instant into the broken and dead body of that little old silver wolf-man who had guided Jack on his way. Then, in another instant and in a puff of cloud, the man's body disappeared and nothing was there.

The great black bird was flying toward the source of the smoke Jack had seen. Now Jack spurred his horse on in that direction.

They came closer and closer to a small stone house. Just as the house really came into view, out of the door burst that evil king with the good king's daughter under his arm. He jumped on his own three-legged horse and took off through the forest.

The bad king did have a lead, but his horse only had three legs. Jack's horse had to be the fastest one the witch had ever bred, and it had all four legs. It was faster!

After a good long race, Jack caught up. He was right on the flank of that old evil king's horse, but he didn't know what to do to get the good king's daughter away from him.

Then Jack's horse started to whinny, "WWhhhununun—wwhhununun! Throw him, sister … throw him, sister …!" That three-legged horse looked back at Jack's horse, and, sure enough, his horse was her sister!

All of a sudden things happened so fast that Jack hardly had time to take it all in.

First, that bad king's horse turned into a three-legged pig, and the bad king got thrown into an oak tree and broke his neck right on the spot.

Then, with a giant crash and pop, the whole forest—trees, ground, grass and all—disappeared. Jack, the king's daughter, and Jack's horse were all falling down and down through the air.

Well, they did fall, down and down and down. Jack could see the world far below as they now fell beside that big tree he had climbed up to start with in order to get to that new land.

Then Jack started getting swimmy-headed, and he passed out. He never did even know when he hit the ground.

The next thing Jack knew, he was trying to sit up. There beside him was the king's daughter, checking herself to see if anything was broken. Over beside both of them that fast horse was just standing and picking grass.

Jack realized that they had landed right back next to the house of that little old woman he had carried the wood for to begin with. He looked around toward where her little house had been, and in its place was the whole big castle where he had met the king's daughter on that foggy night up in the tree.

He also looked around some more, but that big old tree was nowhere to be seen.

Jack and the king's daughter ran to one another. Then they went to the castle and checked it out. It was all there. Even the old servants and cooks and animals had fallen right down with it. Everything was in fine shape to live in.

So Jack and the king's daughter just went ahead and got married and moved into that castle. They didn't need to waste their time being king and queen because everybody around where they lived already knew what they were doing. But they did live there in a happy way for a right long time.

The First Time
Jack Came to America

I bring this collection to a close with one of the strangest stories about Jack that I can remember. It is the natural tale to end with. The specific telling of this story would come whenever we asked, "How did Jack come to live around here anyway? I thought Jack lived over in the old country." I am aware that there are versions of the present story which vary greatly from the one I tell here. I do, however, keep the story as close as possible to the way I remember hearing it. The differences perhaps tell more about the American embodiment of Jack—and especially about the life of my storytelling ancestors—than making it more standardized would do.

There was a time when Jack's daddy had disappeared and nobody knew what had happened to him. Some folks said that he was dead. Others said that he had gone off to a war or to seek his own fortune and that he would come back sometime.

Whatever had happened, he was not there, and Jack and Tom and Will and their mama were having an awful tough time just getting along. Whenever Jack said something about it, his mama always just said, "Unless you can make it on your own, Jack, you can't make it at all!" That might be right, Jack thought, but it was sure nice to have some help.

Anyway, all three boys had jobs in town, and every day they had to get up and walk about four hours to get to work. It was hard to do that and not end up being late by the time you got there.

One day Tom was late getting started and was walking along by himself, just trying to make up for lost time, when he met a little old woman. She was carrying a big load of firewood, and the load had her so bent over that she just couldn't straighten up.

She looked at Tom as he went by and said, "Son, could you help out an old woman in a time of need?" Tom did feel sorry for her, but he was already late for work and just couldn't be any later.

"I'm sorry," he said, "but I just don't have time." He saw that old woman stick her tongue out at him as he went on to town to work, but he never did see her anymore after that.

When Tom got home that day, he told Jack and Will what had happened. Will couldn't believe it. "Why, Tom," he said, "just last week, on a day when I was late, I met the same old woman. I couldn't stop, and she really made a face and ran her tongue out at me as I left."

Jack listened and said, "I don't think I want to tangle up with her. I'm going to try to be on time from now on!"

But as sure as you could guess, not a week passed before Jack slept too late one day. He ended up going to work late and just hurrying as fast as he could to try to make up for lost time.

Before he got halfway to town, he met that little old woman who was all bent over with her load of wood. "Jack," she said just like she knew him, "how about helping me with this wood? Being your daddy's boy, you ought to help me. Neither one of your brothers would."

Jack couldn't figure out what all of this talking was about, but he also couldn't just walk away from somebody who was asking for help. He decided he would just have to get to work late and talk his way out of it the best way he could.

He went over to the old woman and took the load off of her back. Just as he swung it up onto his back, something hit him on the head and knocked him out cold. When he woke up, he was strapped to the back of that old, bent woman, and she carried him as fast as she could walk down a dark passageway and into the very inside of the earth.

She seemed to be plenty strong now, and as Jack struggled he realized that he was tied so tightly that he would never get loose in a thousand years unless she untied him. Down, down, down they went until they finally came out in a huge cavern that was pretty bright from torches and fires. It was all set up to live down there, and Jack saw that she had everything she needed, the same as anybody else right up on top of the earth.

She carried Jack over to where she had a kind of a camp set up. There was a great old black pot—the kind that you would boil clothes in—and it was sitting on three legs over a wood fire.

Behind the pot and beside a big woodpile Jack saw an old man. He kept throwing wood on the fire and stoking it up while it seemed like there was something cooking in the big black pot.

Jack knew that if she put him down, there was no use in running. He didn't have any idea in the world how they had come to get to the place where they were, and, even if he knew the way, they had come so far that Jack would never have the strength to get back home.

It seemed like the old woman knew this, too, because she set Jack down on the ground like she expected him to stay there.

Then she started talking and telling Jack why he was here: "I've been needing some help, Jack, and you're it!

"I started out on the first day of the year, Jack, to gather all of the wisdom in the world. You see, if I can gather every herb and plant that has magic in it over the world and get them all in one year, I can cook the wisdom out and drink it down. Then I will have all of the wisdom in the world for myself."

Jack thought, "She is crazy ... and she is also some kind of witch. But ... I can't get away until I figure out something more than I know now. I'll just have to stay."

Jack looked over at the old man whose job it was to keep the wood split and the fire stoked up. The old man kind of looked familiar to Jack, but beyond that he just couldn't place where he had seen him before. Anyway, the fellow looked terrible from staying down here and working for who knows how long on this fire without a chance to get in the sun or the fresh air either one.

Jack thought that he would probably look just as bad if he had to stay down here very long.

The old witch explained that the black pot was where she was cooking down all the wisdom in the world. She was going up to the earth each day to gather plants and herbs and bringing them back to the black pot. Jack's job would be to stir the pot without stopping so that the wisdom wouldn't stick and burn. This was going to go on until all of the wisdom was cooked out of the whole world.

It was just awful being down there and working so hard day and night. Jack never got to stop stirring that pot. If he ate anything, he had to grab it with one hand and eat while he kept stirring with the other. He and the old man would take turns trying to get something to eat while the old witch was gone. Of course she wouldn't let them completely starve because she did need to keep them alive to stir and put wood on the fire.

The year went on, and each day the old witch would go up to the surface of the earth to gather plants and herbs. At the end of the day she brought them back and added them to the pot. Through the course of the night the pot cooked down until it was empty enough for the next day's batch. One day ran into another, and it seemed like the year would just last forever.

During the last week of the year, the old witch was getting awful frantic. This was the last chance she had to get all of the wisdom of the world and cook it all down. She was running back and forth like mad and was working day and night to try to finish.

What she didn't know is that she had already gathered every plant in the world that had magic or wisdom in it and that the power of all the world's wisdom was already in the very pot that Jack was stirring. What she was getting now was just plain old plants and weeds not worth anything.

On one of her trips up to the earth she stayed for a long time, and the potful of the liquid boiled almost down to nothing. Just as she came back the pot boiled just almost dry, and the last three drops of liquid popped out of the pot and landed on the back of Jack's hand.

Quick as a wink, without even thinking about what he was doing, Jack licked the hot liquid from the back of his burned hand. When he did, the whole world seemed to change.

All of a sudden, he knew exactly which way he would have to go to get back to the surface of the earth. He also suddenly recognized the old man he had been working with as his own long-gone father.

What had happened was that Jack had consumed all of the wisdom of the world in those three drops that he licked from his hand, and there was no wisdom left for the old witch.

Here the witch came, as mad as fire. She had figured out what Jack had done. She picked up the pot and licked the bottom, but there was nothing left there at all for her to take in. She shrieked at Jack and grabbed a piece of firewood. Then she started screaming and swinging that piece of firewood at every-thing in sight.

The witch knocked the black pot over; she knocked fire all over the place. She was screaming at Jack's daddy, and she hit him on the back of the head with the firewood until his eyeballs rolled right down his cheeks.

Then she started after Jack. He ran as fast as he could. Since he had all of the wisdom of the world, he ran exactly the right way to get up to the surface of the earth. The old witch followed him every step of the way, and he couldn't get a lead on her a bit, no matter how hard he ran.

Once they got to the surface of the earth, Jack ran as fast as he could. Still the witch came on as fast as Jack could run away from her.

All of a sudden, Jack figured out that with all of the wisdom of the world he knew all the secrets of shape-changing. This, he thought, might be the very thing to save him from the witch.

So Jack changed himself into a rabbit and outran the witch by a mile.

The only trouble was that the old witch was a shape-changer from way back. As soon as she saw that Jack had changed himself into the rabbit, she changed herself into a fast rabbit dog. In no time she had almost caught up with Jack and was right on the edge of grabbing him in her jaws.

Jack called up all of his new wisdom and figured out how to change himself into a sparrow. Off he flew into the sky, up and away from the old rabbit-dog witch.

As soon as she saw what he had done, she changed herself into a hawk and took off after the sparrow. The hawk circled above the sparrow and took a dive to grasp him in her talons and rip him with her sharp beak.

When Jack saw the hawk diving for him, he again called up the new wisdom he had gained. He thought as fast as he could about what he could turn into that wouldn't hurt him as he fell to the ground.

Suddenly Jack figured it out and turned himself into a grain of corn. He fell right out of the air, too small for the hawk to catch, and lit in the middle of a big cornfield right out of sight.

Jack thought, "Now, this is the thing. Here I am in the middle of a whole field of corn. This is the safest place I could ever be. I'll just lie right here as a grain of corn, and the old hawk witch will never even be able to spot me."

It was a good plan. The hawk landed right close to where Jack was as a grain of corn. The hawk looked around and didn't know what had happened to Jack.

Then the old witch turned herself from a hawk into a chicken. As a chicken, she started right around and around in that field, eating every grain of corn that she could see. Before Jack had a chance even to figure out what to do next, the chicken witch had gobbled him up and swallowed him whole, right down out of sight.

Jack never did know how the old witch knew that she had eaten him, but somehow she did. As soon as Jack was swallowed, she turned herself back into her own natural shape as an old woman, sure that she had done away with Jack and also that she now had all of the wisdom of the world inside herself.

The old witch had, however, turned herself back into a woman before the corn had digested inside the chicken she was when she had eaten it. Instead of being full of all the wisdom in the world, she turned out to be pregnant ... with Jack!

When she realized what had happened, she was absolutely as mad as fire. But she couldn't do anything to Jack without hurting herself, and she was too selfish to hurt herself.

So poor Jack was trapped inside her as a baby waiting to be born. Being a baby not yet born, he didn't have any idea about who or where he was. He just didn't know anything at this time—and wouldn't know anything until he was born.

The old witch vowed and declared that as soon as the baby was born she was going to kill him right on the spot. She just wanted now to get Jack out of her and get it over with. Most of the time she spent just waiting for the day to come when she could get rid of Jack.

However, as time passed, she was not sure that she could kill her own baby with her own hands, and she tried to figure out some other way to get rid of it.

Just about a week before Jack was to be born, the old witch was thinking about what to do with him, when she passed by a place where two men were killing hogs. One of the men was blowing up a hog's bladder to make a ball for his children. This gave the old witch an idea.

She went over to the men and begged them for the biggest hog's bladder. She took the bladder home, blew it up, and hung it in the lean-to behind her house to dry.

A few days later Jack was born.

Without ever even nursing him, the old witch took Jack and cut an opening in that dried hog's bladder. She put the baby inside, sewed up the hole, and sealed the bladder all over with pitch.

Then she threw the bladder into the river, turned her back, and walked away. "I just don't know what happened to that baby," she told herself. "He was crying and alive the last time I saw him." As far as she was concerned, that was that.

The hog's bladder washed down the river with Jack inside. In a few days it ended up floating in the ocean.

Somehow, with all of the wisdom of the world within him, Jack did not die. He lived even without food or air or water and floated in the ocean in that bladder as the currents carried him on and on.

He grew inside that hog's bladder and kept floating there for seven years.

At the end of that time, the bladder washed up on the shore of what Jack thought was a distant land. It turned out that he had floated all the way to America.

When Jack felt the bladder hit the land, he broke out of it and stepped, mostly grown up, right into the sunshine of a new world.

Jack looked around and didn't see anything he knew, or anybody at all. He started to sit down and cry, but then, with all the world's wisdom, he remembered something his mama had told him before he left home on his big adventure to begin with.

He heard her words again: "Unless you can make it on your own, Jack, you can't make it at all."

And so Jack made it. And that is the story of how he came to get to America to begin with, and he's been making it on his own ever since.